STOLEN
GOLD

The Sonrise Farm Series Book 2

Other books by Katy Pistole
The Palomino

KATY PISTOLE

STOLEN GOLD

THE SONRISE FARM SERIES

BOOK • TWO

Pacific Press® Publishing Association
Nampa, Idaho
Oshawa, Ontario, Canada
www.pacificpress.com

Designed by Dennis Ferree
Cover art by Douglas C. Klauba

Copyright © 2002 by
Pacific Press® Publishing Association
Printed in the United States of America
All Rights Reserved

Additional copies of this book are available by calling toll free
1-800-765-6955 or visiting http://www.adventistbookcenter.com

Library of Congress Cataloging-in-Publication data:

Pistole, Katy, 1963-
  Stolen gold/Katy Pistole.
    p. cm. — (Sonrise Farm series ; bk. 2)
  Summary: Jenny's faith is tested when her beloved palomino,
Sunny, proves to be stolen and is returned to an abusive owner,
but her friends and family help her to realize that only God can
help her save Sunny.
  ISBN: 0-8163-1882-4
  [1. Palomino horse. 2. Horses—Training. 3. Animal welfare.
4. Horse farms. 5. Christian Life. 6.Virginia.] I. Title.

PZ7.P64265 St 2002
dc21   2002190395

02 03 04 05 06 • 5 4 3 2 1

Dedication

To the men in my life, Chuck Pistole and Sam Thomsen.
Thank you for showing me the way to Him.
I love you.

Acknowledgments

Thank you more times than I can say to my sweet and
patient husband, Chuck. You are a treasure beyond words.
Many thanks to Fay Strasel of Sunny's Corner Farm.
Your love for Sunny and Roxie is inspirational.
Thank you, Jan Smith, for your friendship, your love,
and your keen eye.
Thank you Elaine and Henry Howard for allowing Sonrise
Farm to exist once again. Thank you to all my horses.
And above all, thank You, Lord, for using my passion for
horses to show me Your passion for me.

And we know that in all things God works for the good
of those who love him,
who have been called according to his purpose.
Romans 8:28

Contents

Chapter One

Sunny tucked her legs under her body as she sailed over the oxer. She flicked her long platinum tail upward to prevent it from pulling the jump down around her.

"Four feet, Sunny girl. You're flyin'," crowed Jenny Thomas, rubbing the mare's golden neck.

The Palomino mare snaked her head, yanking at the reins. Enough with the warm up, let's jump something *big*, she seemed to say. Jenny grinned and glanced over at her trainer, Kathy O'Riley.

"Let me set up a combination," Kathy hollered from across the ring.

Jenny waved acknowledgment and gave Sunny her head. The mare stretched her long neck down, nearly dragging her nose in the bluestone dust.

"Smart girl," Jenny crooned, "stretch that neck." She gazed past the ring at the acres of green grass of Sonrise Farm, remembering the first day she met Sunny. That terrible yet wonderful day. The powerful mare under her looked nothing like the filthy starved creature Jenny had rescued at the auction. The mare who had collapsed and nearly died in the parking lot. *Was that just last summer? So much had happened, it doesn't seem possible.* Just remembering caused Jenny's heart to thump like a drum in her chest.

Jenny's memory drifted over the milestones she and Sunny had reached together. That first incredible ride. Their first show. The day they discovered that Sunny *loved* to jump.

That day—now that was an amazing day. She and Kathy had been hacking through the woods, just taking it easy, when Sunny spied a large fallen tree. She didn't run toward it, but the mare clearly wanted to get closer to it. Jenny had relaxed the reins and given Sunny her head. The mare trotted up to the log and popped over it like it was a ground pole. It was easily 3'9". Jenny lost her stirrups, and nearly flipped backwards out of the saddle. She scrambled frantically and managed to settle herself. She sat up fiddling with the stirrups, then looked up to stare, open mouthed at Kathy. Kathy stared back, as surprised as Jen. They almost fell off their horses laughing at the other's expression.

Jen couldn't help grinning now, thinking about it.

Now she and Sunny were a real team, getting ready to start the A level show circuit. Sunny showed no sign of being over-faced by any of the jumps. They had just cleared four feet like it was nothing.

"Come on, Daydreamer," Kathy yelled. "Let's try that combination."

Jenny nodded, "OK, Boss."

The pair flew over the oxer again. Then the crossrail, then three small cavalettis. Sunny never faltered. Their timing was perfect.

"Lovely," Kathy proclaimed as Sunny came back to earth, bringing a reluctant Jenny along. "Let's quit on that good jump." She shook her head in disbelief. "That mare could jump the moon, Jen."

Jenny smiled and guided Sunny through the gate, playing with Sunny's silvery mane as they walked back to the barn. She could smell the sweet May grass under the mare's feet. It smelled like spring, like rebirth, like resurrection.

Sometimes when Jen was very busy—which seemed nearly always these days—she didn't have time to think. Today her thoughts demanded attention. They flooded her heart and soul, taking her breath away with wonder. *What if Mom had not helped buy Sunny, where would the horse be now? Where would she be?* "There are no coincidences in life," she whispered to Sunny. "We are meant to be together."

Jenny's thoughts flitted to Sunny's registration papers. She had telephoned the Jockey Club two days ago. They had taken all of Sunny's information including the tattoo number inside her upper lip. Jenny was looking forward to researching Sunny's bloodlines. Surely she must have a famous Thoroughbred in her ancestry; perhaps Secretariat or Man O' War. The papers would be delivered soon—maybe today!

She slid off Sunny's side and untacked her. Jenny began singing her favorite song to the mare, "You are my sunshine." Sunny's ears flicked back and forth at the pleasant sound of Jen's voice.

The horse held her face low, to allow Jenny to slide the leather halter over her nose. Sunny released a noisy snort from her nostrils as she relaxed under Jenny's hand. Her eyelids drooped and she dozed in the sun. Jenny threw her arms around the great golden neck and hugged the big mare. She smelled sweaty and sweet.

Sunny turned her head to nuzzle Jen's hair. Her breath smelled like tender young grass. Jenny inhaled the fragrance. "I wish I could bottle your smell. I'd spray it everywhere. We could call it 'Horse Heaven.'"

Jen patted Sunny's face gently then turned to scoop up the saddle from the fence rail. She turned back toward the tack room when Sunny's eyes suddenly snapped open.

Sunny's head jerked up and she stared at the empty driveway. Every muscle was taut and Jen could *see* her mighty heart pounding. "What's wrong, girl?" she asked soothingly. She looked down the driveway but saw nothing.

Sunny reared, rolling her eyes wildly. Jenny quickly unsnapped the safety clip at the mare's halter. *What is going on?* she wondered, reaching for Sunny's halter. The mare went up again, wheeling on her powerful hind legs in the same motion. She exploded into the air, sending up a spray of gravel. The big horse cleared the five-foot gate by a good eight inches.

Jenny could only stare as Sunny streaked to the far end of the ten-acre pasture and melted into a stand of cedars. Her cheek stung and she touched it gently. Her fingers came away wet with blood. Sunny's panicked departure had catapulted a sharp stone at Jenny's face. "Thank goodness it wasn't my eye," she whispered to herself, wiping the blood on her pants leg.

Angry dark clouds rumbled in, hiding the sun. *Could an approaching storm make Sunny crazy? Maybe a tornado is on its way? We don't have tornadoes in Virginia, do we?* Jen wondered, rubbing her bare arms against the sudden chill. She scanned the horizon anxiously.

She heard the cavalcade of cars before she saw them. They crept up the driveway, crunching the gravel beneath the tires. The first car was the Thomas family station wagon, followed closely by a navy Mercedes Benz and three black Ford sedans. A huge navy blue truck with matching stock trailer finished the procession.

Jen started down the hill to greet her parents. *Who are all these folks?* she wondered. Then she saw her dad's anguished expression, and the hair on the back of her neck stood up. Her mom walked toward her, her cheeks wet with tears.

What is going on? Tell me! Did someone die? She wanted to scream. Her cheek stopped stinging. Her lungs were having trouble taking in air. *Is my heart beating?* Yes, there it was, pounding, galloping away.

A uniformed chauffeur opened the back door of the Mercedes and a tall, sharp-featured blond woman emerged. She looked imperiously around Sonrise Farm, her perfectly made-up face frozen in anger. She was attired in wide jodhpurs and high black riding boots. Her long thin fingers were encrusted with large jeweled rings. She held a riding crop in her right hand, which she swung viciously with each step.

Two official looking men appeared out of the black Ford. They flipped their badges and introduced themselves as deputies.

Jenny clutched the rail of the fence helplessly. She didn't know what was going on, but every instinct shrieked at her to climb on Sunny and get away.

"Where is she?" the woman demanded, rudely waving the deputy aside.

"Where is who?" boomed Mr. O'Riley, miraculously appearing behind Jenny.

"My horse, you idiot! Bring her now or I'll have you arrested!" the woman screamed.

"Get off my property," Mr. O'Riley snapped, pointing the way.

"I'm sorry sir, we have a warrant," the older deputy said apologetically. "It seems that you are in possession of Mrs. DuBois's stolen property. We have come to seize one Palomino mare named Gold N' Fire."

Chapter Two

Jen blinked hard. *Surely I'm dreaming,* she assured herself. *This cannot be happening. I bought Sunny, I'm her owner, not this . . . person.*

The deputy stood waiting for someone to go into the field and grab Sunny. No one moved.

"I'll do it myself," Mrs. DuBois shrilled. She grabbed a lead rope with a stallion chain from her Mercedes and stalked into the field. Sunny had hidden herself in the cedars. She stayed motionless until Mrs. DuBois was almost upon her. Then she erupted from her spot and ran straight at the woman. Mrs. DuBois screamed and threw her arms up as she fell to the ground. Sunny ducked nimbly around her and ran bucking and snorting to the fence where Jen stood.

"Hey, Sunny girl, it's OK," Jen soothed, stroking her neck. Sunny's hide dripped with sweat and her muscles twitched all over.

Mr. O'Riley whispered, "Jenny, something is not right. Sunny is acting verra' strange."

Mrs. DuBois slapped the dirt from her jods and approached the mare again. Sunny squealed and actually lashed out with her left hind foot.

"Sunny!" cried Jenny, shocked. "You don't kick!"

"This wretched mare does much more than kick," Mrs. DuBois snarled. "She is the most stubborn, wicked creature I have ever known. Dennis!" the woman screamed at her chauffeur, "Bring me my cell phone, *now.*"

The unfortunate man scurried over with the phone.

Jen watched the woman punch some numbers with her long painted fingernail.

"Hello! Daniel? Is Dr. Vaughn still there? Could you put him on please? Dr. Vaughn, I need you to come and help me with Fire. She is up to her old tricks. Yes . . . I'm at a small farm called . . . what is this place called?"

"Sonrise Farm," Mr. O'Riley said with a scowl. "Mrs. DuBois," he continued, "I would be happy to bring this mare to your farm if it would be easier."

"Sonrise Farm," Mrs. DuBois repeated to Dr. Vaughn. "Thank you, I'll see you in fifteen minutes." The long fingernail punched the phone off. "Nonsense," she sniffed, answering Mr. O'Riley. "I can handle this animal. She just needs to be reminded of who's in charge. Now if someone will put her in a stall until my vet arrives."

Jen walked into Sunny's stall and whistled. The mare hurried toward her and Jen closed the door behind them and stroked the mare's beloved face. "Sunny, I'm sure this is some kind of misunderstanding," she whispered. "I don't know what's going on, but I'm just sure that . . . well, I don't know."

The older deputy hung around outside the stall. Jen turned and caught his eye. His name badge glinted in the sun. Charlie Smith.

"Officer Smith," Jen started, "what's going to happen? I'm sure this is a mistake. I rescued this horse from the meat man at an auction last year. She was so starved she nearly died on the way home."

"I don't know what'll happen, Miss. This woman has proof that this is her horse," Officer Smith shook his head kindly.

Jenny began brushing Sunny's mane. She sang her song, partly to make Sunny comfortable, mostly to keep from bawling. "You are my sunshine, my only sunshine . . . Oh Sunny, I love you. What will happen now?" Her tears burst from her like a torrential flood.

Sunny wrapped her neck around Jen, something she had never done before. It felt like a hug. Jenny threw her arms around Sunny's neck and cried until the mare's silvery mane dripped.

Dr. Vaughn appeared in the doorway, leering unpleasantly. "Hello Fire, it's been a while." Sunny snorted nervously backing away. The vet came after her holding the needle ready. He plunged it into her neck and jumped back out of the way.

Sunny squealed and plunged but quieted at Jen's touch. Moments later a thin string of drool dripped from the mare's bottom lip. Her eyelids grew heavy and she began swaying drunkenly.

"Are we ready in there?" Mrs. DuBois's shrill, hard voice rang out. Sunny's head popped up at the sound of the voice and she appeared more alert. Mrs. DuBois looked into the stall, "Ah, very good, much better . . . come along Fire." She snatched the lead rope from Jen's hand and began walking Sunny toward the navy blue rig.

Jenny read the gold lettering on the side: The DuBois Farm. World Famous Jumpers. Buy and Sell. (703) 555-JUMP.

As they approached the trailer, Sunny balked. She threw her weight backward so suddenly she almost sat down. Every muscle on her powerful body shook. Jenny had never seen such a wild look in the mare's eyes before.

"Come along, Fire," Mrs. DuBois shrieked, feeding the chain over the mare's nose through the halter. Sunny stood still, head up in the air, eyes wild. Jen could see the deep red part of her nostril. Mrs. DuBois jerked on the lead rope causing the chain to bite into Sunny's sensitive face. Sunny reared and almost fell.

Mrs. DuBois grabbed a lunge whip and raised it.

"No!" Jenny screamed. She raced forward just as Mrs. DuBois raised the whip again. Sunny reared and came crashing down. Jenny felt the impact as the huge horse landed on her. Jen lost her footing and everything went black . . .

🐎 🐎 🐎

She was trying to run from the witch but her legs would not move. Jenny pried her eyelids loose. They seemed glued together. The room was swirling. The hag leaned over her triumphantly.

It wasn't a hag. It was a nurse. *Where am I?* she wondered, feeling dazed. Her lips were dry, her tongue felt like a mattress. The bright white walls were unfamiliar. *The smell . . . what is that smell? Alcohol? Formaldehyde?*

She could hear Mom and Dad far away. *Am I in a hospital? Why? Where is Sunny?*

"Sunny!" She raised her leaden arm to rub her aching forehead. Mom was instantly at her side. "What happened?" Jenny croaked.

"Your horse, I mean Sunny, fell on you," Mom whispered *so* gently.

"How?"

"What do you remember?" Dad asked quietly.

"Not much," Jen responded. "The last thing I saw was Sunny hiding in some trees in the pasture. Then this witch was trying to eat me . . . I think that part was a nightmare."

"Sweetheart," whispered Dad leaning forward. "Sunny has been claimed by someone. She belongs to a woman named Mrs. Vanessa DuBois. She was stolen from the DuBois Farm eighteen months ago. The Jockey Club notified the police when you called them with Sunny's information.

"Mrs. DuBois came to claim Sunny. Sunny seemed to go crazy whenever the woman came near her. Mrs. DuBois had to call her vet to come and sedate her. They began hitting Sunny to get her on the trailer. Sunny reared, lost her balance, and fell on you. You hit your head on the corner of Mrs. DuBois's trailer."

A frozen hand clutched her throat. "You mean *I* caused this by calling the Jockey Club?" she choked, wishing she could disappear.

"Jenny . . ." whispered Mom. "You wouldn't want to keep a stolen horse. I know it's awful, but Sunny belongs to someone else."

Jenny buried her head in the pillow and wept.

"She has a concussion, keep her quiet for a week, and *no* horseback riding for three weeks," Dr. Stone commanded as Jenny's parents took her home from Loudoun Memorial Hospital. Dr. Stone patted Jen's back gently. "I'll see you back here in ten days for a recheck young lady. If you have any questions or any new symptoms, call immediately."

Jen nodded silently as she lowered herself into the cold seat of the wheelchair.

Dad wheeled her out and Mom waited with her under the awning while he brought the car. Jen stared at her folded hands, trying to ignore the questioning sympathetic glances from passers-by. *Why? Why? Why?* The question pulsed with each heartbeat.

"I don't feel like riding anyway," Jen assured her folks as they drove home.

"Kathy called," Mom said looking over her shoulder at Jen. "You should call her back and let her know you're home."

Jen turned her face away to stare out the window. *How can I call Kathy? What am I supposed to say? I must have done something to make God angry with me. Why else would He punish me this way? Life without Sunny . . . I can't do it. I won't do it. I've got to figure out a way to see her again.*

"Kathy? Hi, it's Jenny. Oh fine, I guess. Yeah, no riding for three weeks. I don't know what I want to do. I just got home. I'll call ya' next week? OK . . . thanks, bye."

Jenny curled up in her bed, hugging her favorite squishy pillow. Angry thoughts crashed over her like waves on the shore.

Why did this happen? I should have known it was too good to be true. I don't deserve to be treated this way, God. Why would You take Sunny away? You can't be the God I trusted. I gave my riding to You. What do You want from me?

The more Jen dwelled there, the angrier she became. By the time her mom called her for dinner, she was in a dark mood.

"I made your favorite," Mom announced. "Veggie alphabet soup."

Jen pushed the succulent carrot chunks around with her spoon. "I'm not hungry," she whined. Her own voice sounded strange and heavy. "Can I go back to bed, Mom? My head feels weird."

Mom glanced at Dad with a worried look. "Sure, I'll check on you in a little while."

Jenny heard their whispers as she padded down the hall. She walked carefully to keep from jarring her tender head. She curled up in bed and closed her eyes.

Sunny was flying over the course like silk. The jumps were enormous. They were an unstoppable team. They approached the last jump at a full gallop. It was a water jump, Jenny's favorite. As soon as Sunny took off Jenny knew they were in trouble. The water fell out from under them to reveal a steep cliff. It was too late. They were over the edge. Jenny hauled helplessly on the reins, screaming as they plunged into a bottomless ravine.

The scream woke her parents and herself. Her long blond

hair clung to her sweaty face. Jen's head clanged like a gong. She barely made it to the bathroom before throwing up.

"I'm calling Dr. Stone," Mom cried.

"No, I'm all right," Jen moaned, collapsing on the cold tile floor of the bathroom.

They sat together in the sterile waiting room of the hospital. Dr. Stone appeared, looking disheveled and worried. "Let's keep her overnight, for observation," he suggested. "She may just be dehydrated. I'll give her an I.V. with fluids and we'll do another brain scan first thing in the morning."

The scan revealed a cerebral contusion buried deep in Jen's brain. *Just more proof that God is mad at me,* she concluded.

Chapter Three

She looks like a dried apple, Jen thought, studying her homebound teacher's face. She was supposed to be doing math, but her eyes kept returning to the wrinkled face of Mrs. Peabody.

"Do you have a question, dear?" the teacher finally asked.

"Oh . . . no, I'm just thinking," Jenny mumbled, embarrassed.

Jen's prison sentence was almost over. She had been at home for four weeks. No horses, no friends. *In some ways it's almost over, in other ways it's just starting,* she reminded herself. *Life without Sunny is going to be a new kind of prison.*

"If you can finish these last three pages of geometry, you'll be on track with your classmates and ready to start school on Monday," Mrs. Peabody said, gently nudging Jen back to math. "Wouldn't it be fun to finish the year with your friends? You'll just have one week of school left. Assuming your scan goes well today, and I'm sure it will."

Jen sighed. *Will anything be fun again?* she asked herself. "Yes, ma'am," she answered her teacher.

Jenny's scan showed that the contusion had disappeared. "Praise God," Mom whispered as she hugged Jen.

I'm not sure I'm ready for school, Jenny thought.

"You may begin riding again, Miss Thomas," Dr. Stone pronounced. "No jumping or galloping. You cannot take another head injury right now. You may experience dizziness or even fainting, so be careful. If you feel dizzy, get off the horse and come straight back here. Do you understand?"

"I'll be careful," she promised. But inside she was thinking, *How can I ride any horse but Sunny? It will never be the same.* Jen's heart ached, each beat echoing painfully in her chest.

"Be joyful always; pray continually; give thanks in all circumstances, for this is God's will for you in Christ Jesus. This is what Paul told the early believers."

Jenny's face burned as she listened to Pastor Jeff reading from 1 Thessalonians. *How can I be joyful and thankful now?* she wondered bitterly. *What kind of a God would take Sunny away and then tell me to be happy about it? There is no way.* Jenny shut her ears and heart off. She spent the rest of the service scheming about Sunny. *How can I see her again?*

The bus picked Jenny up at the corner on Monday morning. Her best friend Tessa Silversteen shrieked and cleared a spot on her seat. "You're back," she cried, "I've missed you. Are you all right? I saw this thing on TV about Sunny. Did you know she'd been stolen when you bought her?"

Jenny's dark expression made Tessa stop rattling on. "Of course I didn't know she'd been stolen," Jen hissed, her eyes filling with big, fat, tears. She couldn't stop them. They escaped, plopping onto her book bag and rolling off into her lap.

"I'm sorry, Jen," Tessa apologized. "I guess I wasn't thinking."

"What channel was it on?" Jen sniffled. It would be heartbreaking to watch, but she felt compelled to see the news clip.

Tessa shrugged. "I dunno. But I'll find out. My mom will know. She seemed *really* interested, from a legal standpoint."

"What do you mean?" Jen asked.

Tessa hesitated, then launched into an explanation. "My mother said that it was an interesting case because you had proof that you had purchased Sunny from the guy at the auction. The auction house that sold Sunny and the farmer who brought Sunny to be sold are under investigation."

"Why?"

"Because Sunny is a valuable show jumper."

Now Jen was really confused. "How could she be a show jumper? We hadn't even done a rated show!"

Tessa squinted at Jenny suspiciously. "Do you *watch* TV at your house?"

"Not much," Jen admitted. "I had no idea this would be on the local news."

"Jenny," Tessa hissed, "This isn't *local* news. It's international! Sunny's real name is Gold N' Fire. She's a Grand Prix jumper imported from England. There are only, like, three Palomino Thoroughbred mares in the whole world. She was insured for over two million bucks! I don't know how you got away with keeping her for as long as you did. Mrs. DuBois said the horse just "disappeared" eighteen months ago. She had filed a statement with the animal warden, but didn't tell them what the horse was worth. My mom says it sounds like fraud."

"What does *that* mean," Jen asked, her head pounding with all this new information.

"Well," whispered Tessa, with a furtive glance around, "my mom says the story doesn't add up. If you lost a horse worth that much, you'd tell everyone. Right? So why didn't Mrs. DuBois file a police report? Why didn't she contact the newspapers and television stations? Sunny has been right under her nose the entire time. You weren't hiding her. You were *showing* her. My mom thinks Mrs. DuBois didn't *want* to find Sunny because she could collect the insurance. Two million bucks is a lot of cash!"

Tessa explained how Sunny got to the auction. "The police traced the chain of people back to a farmer who found her in his field. Sunny was hanging out with his cattle. He brought her to the auction because he figured she was just some old nag who had been turned away by her owners. You remember what she looked like. The farmer said she had looked that way since the day she showed up at his farm. He never thought to look in her mouth to see if she was tattooed. He had no idea she was even a Palomino. How did a horse like Sunny wind up starved to near death, hangin' out with a bunch of cows?"

"So," Jenny croaked, "do you know where Sunny is now?"

28

"She is at The DuBois Farm, about five miles from here."

Jenny felt sick and happy at the same time. *Sunny is so close, but she might as well be 5,000 miles away!* The thought of seeing Vanessa DuBois again filled Jenny with anger and fear.

Before long, Jen's luck seemed to change. When she boarded the school bus on Monday, the last week of school, she was greeted by a smug Tessa. "Guess what, Jen," Tess whispered loudly. She waved Jen closer, looked around and whispered softly into Jen's ear. "We've got a friend who has a horse at The DuBois Farm. She is willing to sneak us in. You could check things out."

"Really? *We* have a friend? Who?"

"You know—Shannon Lockhart."

"Shannon, that snobby girl who made fun of me at horse camp last year? That Shannon? And what do you mean *sneak?*"

"Well," Tessa whispered, "Mrs. DuBois doesn't allow guests at her barn so we'll have to be sure to stay out of her way. And yes, it's the same Shannon. Do you want to see Sunny or not?"

Jen's heart leapt at the words. *I would do anything to see Sunny again.* "What about my parents?" Jen hesitated. "They won't let me sneak around like that."

"No problem," Tessa said, shaking her dark curls. "Tell them you're coming to my house, or wait, tell them that you're . . . hangin' out with me. Yeah. That's true, and we just won't say *where* we're hanging out."

"OK . . . that *might* work. I'll try it tonight."

"Mom, Dad, can I go to Tessa's house after school tomorrow?"

Mom frowned with surprise for a moment. "Jen, we don't really know Tessa's parents. I'm not sure . . ."

"Oh please, Mom, I've missed her so much and she's gonna help me . . . you know . . . catch up on everything. Please!" Jenny did her best puppy dog impression, with big sad eyes.

Mom looked at Dad. "What do you think?" she asked.

Dad stared doubtfully at Jen's silly expression. "Well . . . I . . . OK, Jen, but you need to call home when you get to Tessa's house. You may stay for a couple of hours."

"Great! Thanks, Dad." Jen picked up her fork and stared down at her food. *Funny,* she thought, *I've kind of lost my appetite.*

She overheard her parents talking about her after dinner. They obviously thought she was in her room. They were huddled together at the kitchen table discussing. "It's the first thing she's been excited about since Sunny was taken," Mom said softly.

"I know," Dad agreed. "It just worries me a little."

"Well, let's pray for her together. God sees what we can't. He will protect her."

I don't need protecting, Jenny thought. *I can take care of myself.* She slipped back into her room to finish her essay for social studies.

Jen woke the next morning with butterflies in her stomach. Her hands actually tingled with excitement. She shook them out on her way to the kitchen.

"Hey, sweetheart," Mom said with a smile. "How did you sleep?"

"Great." Jenny ducked her head to avoid eye contact. *I'm not doing anything wrong,* she argued with herself. *Mom doesn't need to know where I am all the time. Why do I feel so guilty? I need to do it this way. Mom and Dad would never understand. This is the only way.* Jen nibbled at her breakfast and gathered her backpack.

"Aren't you ready a little early?" Mom asked, glancing at the kitchen clock as Jenny headed out the door.

"Yeah, I guess." Jen shrugged. "I'm gonna study while I wait for the bus."

"All right then, have a great day. I'll pick you up at Tessa's house around five."

"Great! Thanks, Mom." Jenny turned and fled to the bus stop, her heart pounding. *I can't wait to see Sunny,* she thought, imagining the reunion. Jenny's thoughts swirled around her like billows of curling smoke. She was surprised by the school bus.

Tessa cleared a spot next to her and Jenny plopped down. "How did it go?" Tessa chirped.

"Fine, I guess. I have never lied to my parents before. It feels weird."

"You're not really lying," Tessa said. "You are omitting a small detail. That's all."

Jen nodded. "Well, my mom is picking me up at your house at five."

"Eww." Tessa scowled. "That's gonna be tight. We'll have to hurry."

Jenny spent the endless day imagining seeing Sunny again. She could see the mare leaning down and whickering softly. Jenny could almost *feel* Sunny's warm sweet breath on her face.

"Jenny Thomas, would you like to try this problem?"

It was Mrs. Heyne, the math teacher, holding out a piece of chalk. Jen coughed and nodded her head. She rose mechanically and stood frozen at the blackboard. *What am I supposed to be doing?* She looked frantically at Mrs. Heyne.

"Were you listening, Jenny?" Mrs. Heyne questioned gently.

"No, ma'am," Jen admitted, feeling miserable.

"Who can help Jennifer with this problem?"

Jenny passed the chalk to Will, the tall guy who sat in the front row. She slithered into her seat, vowing to pay attention for the rest of the day.

Chapter
Four

Tessa's house was a condo and it was incredible. High cathedral ceilings and huge arched windows overlooked a small lake where four swans swam. The furniture was white leather with huge pillows everywhere. It all looked brand new.

Jenny thought about the brown plaid sofa at home—the one with the blanket thrown over the hole in the back. She had never thought about that sofa before, but now she couldn't seem to *stop* thinking about it.

Tessa pulled out some clothes for them. The britches were nicer than Jenny's show britches. "We've got to look the part," Tessa said seriously. "This is a fancy barn. The board is $1,000.00 a month."

Jenny pulled the clothes on quickly while Tessa grabbed several pairs of boots. None of the boots actually fit, but Jen managed to cram her feet into the last pair. They curled her toes, but she didn't care. *I'm going to see Sunny!* she kept thinking. Nothing else mattered.

The girls grabbed a granola bar and headed out the door. Tessa stopped outside to lock the deadbolt. There was a cab waiting outside the sliding door of the foyer. The girls waved goodbye to Stan, the burly security guard, then Jenny slid into the taxi after Tessa.

"Where to today, Miss Tessa?" the cab driver asked.

"We're going to Shannon's house," Tessa replied. "I'll tell you how to get there."

It was like a strange dream. She was in a taxi, on her way to Shannon Lockhart's house. The only other time she remembered being in a taxi was when Grandpa Thomas died and they flew to Ohio for the funeral. They had taken a cab from the airport to Grandma and Grandpa's house, then again from the airport in Virginia, to home. It seemed like Tessa rode in this cab a lot.

"Here we are. Thanks, Jim." Tessa handed the cabbie some money and they hopped out. Jenny stared at the house they were parked in front of. It looked like a mansion. "Is the barn here?" she asked Tessa.

"No silly, this is Shannon's house. She is going to *sneak* us into her barn. Mrs. DuBois doesn't like strangers hanging around. If we show up in a cab, we'll never get past the front gate. We need to ride with Shannon."

Shannon's driver was named Bill. Jen sat in the back of a Jaguar for the first time in her life. The car purred up and out the driveway. Ten minutes later they stopped at a huge black iron gate. Jen and Tessa slipped under a blanket and lay on the floor. A security guard waved them on after seeing Shannon's driver. As the car rolled smoothly up a long tree-lined driveway, Jenny peeked out.

"You can come out now. It's safe," Shannon announced. The car slowed and pulled into an asphalt parking lot. Jenny climbed out of the car in a daze. *Are we in the right place?* she

wondered. The barns were white with navy trim. The acres of manicured fields were neatly fenced with white three-board fencing. There were curtains in some of the windows and flowers everywhere. It didn't look like a barn, except for the horses. Even they looked perfect. Jenny looked around, her mind whirling. *Sunny! I'm here to find Sunny.*

Shannon began to give them a tour of the place. Jen's feet were hurting from the cramped boots. She felt edgy and cranky. *Where is that blue Mercedes?* she kept wondering.

"There are three barns," Shannon began, " the upper barn, the lower barn, and the indoor arena barn. We're in the lower barn. Each barn houses twenty-four horses. The indoor arena is just over there. I'm on the waiting list to get a stall in the indoor arena barn." Shannon looked knowingly at Jen.

Jenny shrugged her shoulders and looked to Tessa. "What does she mean by that?" she asked.

Tessa rolled her eyes. "The indoor arena is where all the 'important' people keep their horses."

"If you see Mrs. DuBois's dark blue Mercedes, I don't know you," Shannon sniffed.

That settled it for Jenny. "Let's go," she said to Tessa, ignoring Shannon. "Sunny might be in the indoor arena." The two girls abandoned the surprised Shannon and ran toward the big building.

"Hey! Wait for me," Shannon called.

They spent the next hour searching every stall. There was no sign of Sunny.

"What are we going to do?" Jen complained to Tessa. I'm almost out of time."

"Let's ask someone," Tessa suggested. "Look, there's a groom. Let's ask him."

Jen approached the groom shyly. "Um, excuse me, could you tell me where I might . . . uh, I mean, have you seen . . ."

The young man turned around to face her. "I'm sorry, ma'am, do you need help with something?"

Did he just call me ma'am? Jen wondered. She drew in a breath. "Yes, I'm looking for a Palomino Thoroughbred mare."

The groom stepped back as though she had waved a weapon. "No, ma'am! I have not seen anything!" He spun around and marched off quickly.

Jenny stared after him. *He knows where she is . . .*

Shannon's whiny voice pierced the stillness. "We've got to go, and I didn't even get to ride."

Jenny stared out the window of the Jaguar as it slid down the long driveway. *Why did he react that way? What is happening at this place?* Tears slid down her face. *I didn't find Sunny.*

It was driving her crazy. *I have to know,* she thought. *I have got to find her. That groom knows something, but what?*

"Jenny, are you all right?" Mom asked as she set the plate of spaghetti down.

"Yeah. I'm fine. Why?" Jen answered, picking up her fork.

"You just seem to have a lot on your mind."

"Oh . . . no. Just school ending and everything," she lied, twirling saucy noodles around her fork.

Dad raised his eyebrows. "Shall we say grace?"

"Oops. Sorry, I forgot," she apologized.

36

They ate the meal in silence. Jenny couldn't wait to escape to her room. She was actually thankful for the homework that allowed her to avoid her folks. The excitement of seeing Sunny had vanished, leaving a dark hole of guilt in its place. Now she couldn't even tell them how crummy she felt and why. *I will never lie to them again,* she swore to herself.

The next morning, the bus arrived and Tessa had more news. "Hey, Shannon says we can go back to her barn. She wants you to help her with her horse. Her trainer is suddenly too busy to give her lessons. Shannon's horse is supposedly this great ex-race horse. She can't even get on him."

Tessa was grinning like this was the best news in the whole world. "How am I supposed to do that?" Jen huffed, staring at her.

"I guess you'll have to tell your folks about Shannon and her predicament. They don't need to know that it's Mrs. DuBois's Farm. Shannon is counting on you, Jen. You are getting a reputation as a rider."

"Really?" Jen felt a swell of pride. "What about getting in? I thought no guests were allowed."

"We'll need to keep our eyes peeled," Tessa explained patiently, as though speaking to a very young child. "It is a big place, so just keep your head low and fit in. Mrs. DuBois is almost never there anymore and the security guard stays at the gate. Look Jen, if you are serious about finding Sunny you need to do this. Just *use* Shannon to get in."

"All right," Jenny said, feeling not at all right.

"Absolutely not!" Dad reacted just the way Jenny thought he would. "You need to be really careful after your head injury. I don't want you riding any 'difficult' horses. Shannon has to get someone else to help her."

"Daa-ad," she moaned. "She doesn't have anyone else. How about if I just help her from the ground. I won't get on."

Dad looked at Mom for help. "What should we do here?" he asked.

Mom replied, "I trust her. If Jenny says she won't get on, I believe she won't get on."

Jen felt another twisting barb of guilt. *Trust. She trusts me.*

"All right," Dad relented. "If I hear that you have even walked around the ring on Shannon's horse . . ."

"I know, I know," Jen replied. "I promise Daddy. No riding. I'll just help her from the ground. I guess I'll be giving her a riding lesson." That sounded strange, seeing how Shannon had been at the Sonrise Farm riding camp with Jenny last year.

Mom smiled. "It's nice of you to help your friend."

Really nice, thought Jen. *What would you think of me if you knew why I'm being so nice?*

"Shannon, keep your heels out of his sides. No wonder he's running off with you—you keep telling him to go," Jen hollered from across the ring.

"I'm not telling him anything," Shannon wailed, clutching the reins to her chest fearfully.

Tessa watched from the bleachers with an amused smirk on her face.

"Let me put you on the lunge line," Jenny shouted. "Bring him over here."

Shannon clung to the horse's mane with one fist while pulling the rein awkwardly with the other. Her horse meandered drunkenly in Jen's direction. Jenny stroked the chestnut neck. "What's his name again?" she asked.

"Simon Says," Shannon replied, "but we call him The Frog."

Jenny frowned. "Frog? Why Frog?"

"Because he hops all over the place," Shannon replied sheepishly.

Jenny shrugged and clipped the lunge line onto The Frog's bridle. "I want you to walk around me and shrug your shoulders up and down." Shannon did. As she did, her shoulders relaxed. Jenny smiled, remembering the hours of lunge line work she had done with Kathy as her instructor. *Kathy! I need to call Kathy.* She made a mental note to do that as soon as she got home. "Tessa!" Jen commanded. "Come here!"

"What?" asked Tessa, jogging toward the center of the ring. She ducked under the lunge line and slowed to walk.

"Hold this," said Jenny. "Keep her walking around shrugging her shoulders. I'll be back. Remind her to keep her heels down and out of Froggy's sides." And she sprinted toward the indoor ring where she had seen the groom the other day.

He was there, mucking a stall.

"Umm, excuse me . . ." she began.

He stopped working to look up. "Yes, ma'am, how can I help you?" He turned pale as he recognized her face.

She walked into the stall. "I need your help," she whispered urgently. "I'm looking for my horse . . . I mean *a* horse. She's a big Palomino mare."

"I don't know anything about any Palomino," he insisted staring intently at the ground. "I just work here, mucking, feeding, and minding my own business."

"I know you know something," she huffed. "I'm desperate. I *need* to see her."

"And I *need* this job," he replied. "Good day, ma'am." He nearly tripped over himself running from the stall.

Great, Jenny thought. *Now what?*

She shuffled, dejected, back toward the ring where Shannon and Tessa waited. A huge, twisted maple root caused her to stumble and nearly fall. As she steadied herself against the rough, tall trunk, she saw something out of the corner of her eye. It was a dark brown building nearly in the woods. It looked like a miniature barn. *What a strange little place. Why didn't I notice it before? Why is it brown when everything else is white? It's almost like it's not supposed to be seen.*

Approaching the strange little barn, she realized it was surrounded by a high chain link fence, topped with barbed wire. It looked like prison fencing. The barn itself was tucked in a hollow, the front was a normal height, the back set into the hill. *This is a bank barn,* she realized. *I've never seen one before. Why is it surrounded with barbed wire? I'll ask Shannon,* she decided.

"It's a quarantine barn," Shannon explained back at the arena. "When horses come from other countries, they are sometimes kept separate for a few weeks. It protects the other horses from foreign diseases. I've never seen it used."

"Hmm," Jen whispered. "I'll have to check it out."

"What?" Shannon asked, looking startled.

"Oh, nothing," Jenny said with a smile. "Let's get back to work."

Shannon is really making progress, Jenny thought, as she watched Shannon ride The Frog. "You look nice, Shannon," she said out loud. "Much more relaxed."

Shannon rode for ten more minutes, then slid off The Frog. "I haven't ridden him for that long ever!" she beamed.

"Great, congrats," Jen said quickly. "Why don't you go and get him untacked. I'll wait here." As soon as Shannon walked away, Jenny ducked to the left and scurried toward the quarantine barn. She found a little thicket of bushes and scrunched back into them. *Perfect view.*

Just then, the groom walked up to the gate of the quarantine barn. He glanced around him, then opened the combination lock. Jen watched him until he closed the huge sliding door behind him. She tried to peer into the belly of the building but it was dark inside. *She's in there, I know it. But why?*

Chapter Five

"Kathy called again," Mom said, looking sideways at Jenny while she folded clothes on their shabby living room sofa.

"OK," Jen murmured, face planted in a book. "I'll call her back."

"Whatcha' reading with such interest?" Mom asked.

Jen held up the paperback. *Training Secrets for Jumpers,* she read from the cover. "It was written by Kathy's grandfather. He had some great ideas."

"Are you thinking about training horses now?" Mom asked.

Jenny smiled. "Well, until I can ride, yes, I guess I am."

Mom smiled back. "Good. I think that's a great idea. You can probably help some folks."

Help Shmelp, Jen thought. *I need to find a way to get to that barn every day. Eventually I'll catch that groom as he's going in, and I'll convince him to help me. It'll work, I know it will.*

By the end of the week, Shannon and The Frog were doing really well. Jen was so distracted by the quarantine

42

barn that she was startled to see them walking nicely together in the ring. She thought for a moment that they were another horse and rider and that she'd lost her only student. She tried to focus on their lesson for the day.

"Think about lying on a warm beach," Jen instructed Shannon. "Relax your shoulders and close your leg slightly. Don't think about trotting. Just close your leg."

It was a trick Kathy used all the time to keep riders from becoming fearful. It worked. Shannon and The Frog began trotting around the ring. No bucking or hopping.

"Yeah," Jenny shouted. "Now think heavy, stop posting and pull gently."

The Frog stopped so suddenly that Shannon had to adjust her seat.

"See, you can ride him," Jenny called out with a laugh. "You just needed to get rid of your stiff back and hands."

Shannon was beaming. "I never thought I'd be able to trot on him. My other trainer would just start yelling and then I couldn't do anything. Thank you, Jenny."

"It's OK," Jen answered. *I'm so glad my trainer never yells at me,* she thought gratefully. *Kathy! I didn't call Kathy. I need to do that as soon as I get home.*

Jenny looked over her shoulder just as the groom walked out of the upper barn. He carried a bucket in each hand and some flakes of hay under his arm. He glanced around then headed straight for the quarantine barn. "Shannon, walk around for a minute, I'll be right back." She turned and sprinted toward her hiding place.

"Whaaat?" Shannon wailed.

Jen ducked down behind the bush. The groom fiddled with the lock for a moment, opened it, and hung the chain on the gate. *Thank you,* Jenny thought. He looked around, then ducked inside the big sliding door, leaving it slightly open. Jenny ran for the gate and slipped through. Then she bolted for the barn door. She peeked in and turned sideways to slide through the narrow opening. Her belt caught the door and caused it to bounce against the doorframe. The groom dropped the buckets with a clatter.

"What are you doing?" he hissed, his eyes terrified.

"You have some horses in here—don't you?" she demanded.

He grabbed her elbow with strong fingers and propelled her to the door. "Look, you don't know what's going on here," he insisted. "If anyone sees you, I'll lose my job. If I lose my job, these horses will die."

"Tell me what's going on here," she whispered through clenched teeth, "and I'll help you." She wrenched her arm out of his grasp and rubbed the purpling spots.

"I don't need some girl helping me," he said with a grimace.

Jenny changed her tactics. "You said horses—how many horses are in here?"

The groom groaned. "None of your business."

Then Jenny couldn't help it. The tears came pouring down her face. "I just want to see her, just once," she tried to say.

The young man buried his face in his hands, then stared at her. "I'm gonna lose my job," he muttered. "Stay here for a second, let me check it out." He left her there and poked his head out of the door to scan the horizon. "All right, come on," he growled.

They entered the bowels of the barn and the stench of old urine rolled up to burn Jenny's nose. She poked the lower part of her face into her shirt to filter out the stink. She ran to the first stall and looked in. Both doors were closed and bolted so Jen looked through the feed slot. A thin colt stood in the dark corner, peering fearfully at her. He looked to be two, maybe three years old.

She kept going. The next stall was larger and darker. Jen could hear something inside but her eyes had not adjusted to the dank innards of the bank barn. Jen stared through the feed slot until she saw spots. She blinked hard and sighed impatiently. Her sigh brought an eruption of frantic activity from the stall.

Jenny could only make out a white blaze. Then she saw her and gasped. It was Sunny, thin and terrified, struggling to get as far away from the person at the stall door as possible. She had large, crusty wounds on her shoulders and flanks from trying to climb the walls.

"Sshhh, Sunny girl, its me," Jenny said in her most soothing voice.

The mare stopped plunging.

"That's right. It's OK. I'm here now."

Sunny pricked her ears and looked for a moment like the Sunny Jen remembered.

Jenny reached over to open the stall door and the sound threw the mare back into panic.

The groom locked his fingers around Jen's arm. "Are you nuts?" he growled. "This horse is insane. She would kill you in a heartbeat."

Jenny flew back to the feed slot. "Sshhh, Sunny, its me. Me girl, I'm not going to hurt you." Sunny rolled her eyes back until the whites showed. Then the mare began flinging her head and banging it hard against the walls of the stall. Her hide darkened as sweat lathered over her twitching body. She seemed intent upon killing herself.

Jenny fled from the dungeon into the bright sun filled afternoon, sobbing uncontrollably.

"Look," the groom said. "I don't know what your problem is. I was hired to take care of these horses. You are making my job impossible."

Jen opened her mouth, but no words came out. Everything went dark as she slid to the ground.

Someone was slapping her face. How did she get outside?

"Wake up, please wake up," Jenny heard desperation in the voice. Her eyes fluttered. "Oh thank heaven," he whispered. "Please wake up, you're going to get me in so much trouble."

She forced her eyes open. The clean air felt good in her lungs. The groom peered into her face with apparent concern. Then she heard his words: "You are going to get *me* in so much trouble . . ."

"Great," she shouted, coming completely awake. "All you care about is your hide, your precious job. How can you stand by and let those horses starve? How much could she pay you to help her do that?"

"You don't understand," he mumbled. "It's not the money. You wouldn't understand."

"Try me," she shouted.

"Look, Mrs. DuBois is my Aunt Vanessa. She took me in when no one else would. If I don't help her, she'll never break these horses."

"This is *not* how you 'break' horses. This is how you torture horses," the words streamed like a torrent from her lips.

They stared at each other like lions for several moments.

"My name is Daniel," the groom finally sighed. " My parents live in California, in a big house near the ocean. I ran into some trouble out there. My parents were ready to send me to a juvenile detention place when Aunt Vanessa offered me this job. If I mess it up, it's back I go. I can't go back, I just can't."

"What did you do?" asked Jen.

"I took my dad's Porsche for a drive," Daniel spoke quietly, with a far away look. "I had driven it before, with permission. I picked up some friends and well . . . I let Joey drive. Big mistake. He crashed it in a tunnel near Malibu. We weren't wearing seat belts. Joey was hurt pretty badly. He almost died.

"My dad had called the police. He thought the car had been stolen. Then the hospital called to tell him where I was. My dad was so mad he was ready to press charges against me. Joey's folks tried to sue my dad." Daniel's face contorted in pain. "Anyway, it was a real mess and Aunt Vanessa's idea seemed like the best one of the bunch. I am grateful to her."

"So, you are here," Jen replied, trying to sort out the details, "working for free for your aunt because she is teaching you how to be a horse trainer? And you've been here for how long?"

"Two years," he replied.

"And you've learned . . . what? Mrs. DuBois's method of cruelty training?"

"She's not cruel," he argued. "She's firm. These are not normal horses. These are dangerous, difficult horses."

"I rescued Sunny a year ago from the meat man," Jen explained. "She nearly died in the parking lot. She was never 'dangerous or difficult' for me. I love her and I want her back. I need to help her. Will you help me?"

Daniel stared at her like she was crazy. "Do you know who you're talking about? This horse is worth two million dollars. Are you gonna buy her? How are *you* gonna get her back? Go home, girl. This is too big for you."

Jenny stared back. "She's not worth two million right now. You can't even touch her."

"No," he agreed. "Not right now. She'll have to find a way to collect the insurance money again."

"How will she do that?" Jen asked, feeling the hair stand up on the back of her neck.

"Nothing. I shouldn't even be talking to you," he huffed. "This is bigger than me *or* you. I have it worked out. I'm feeding them. It's under control."

Jenny glared at him. "Feeding them what? A handful of grain and a flake of hay?"

Daniel glared back, "She feeds them well . . . when they're good."

"What?" Jenny couldn't believe her ears. "They get fed when they're good? What is being good?"

Daniel sighed heavily. "Aunt Vanessa is a horse trainer. You're not. She imported Gold N' Fire from England because she wanted to own and train a world famous jumper.

Fire was already well on her way to being the best. I never saw a horse that loved to jump like Fire. After Aunt Vanessa got the horse to the States, Fire went crazy. She became dangerous and just plain bad. She dumped Aunt Vanessa at a big show, on live TV. My aunt was happy when the mare disappeared two years ago because she got the insurance money.

"Now that Fire is back, Aunt Vanessa has to repay the insurance company. She is really mad about that. Aunt Vanessa has 90 days to prove the mare is still worth two million. After that, the insurance company will pull the policy. Aunt Vanessa is determined to collect the money one way or another. Either Fire will submit, or my Aunt will figure out another way to collect. I really think my aunt hates that mare."

Jen's mouth hung open as she listened to the stream of information flow from Daniel's mouth. " And that's Sunny's colt?"

"Yeah," he nodded. "He's just as nuts as the mare. Unmanageable, a real killer."

A loud car horn blared from the parking lot. "Daniel!" The shrill voice of Mrs. DuBois cut through the air like a knife. "I need help. Get over here. Now!"

Dan froze for a moment. "Hide," he hissed, turning pale. "She'll kill me if she finds you here."

Jen glanced wildly around. There was nowhere to hide. Except back inside the barn. She ran back into the blackness and promptly collided with a tack trunk. "Owww," she groaned softly.

The sound sent a flurry of activity from Sunny's stall.

"Sorry, girl," Jen whispered. "Didn't mean to scare you."

Jenny spied the ladder to the hayloft. It was rickety and the wood was rotten but she climbed it quickly. The air was worse up there, hot, stuffy, smelling of old urine *and* moldy hay. The ceiling was so low Jenny had to crouch. Masses of cobwebs tickled her face and hair. The floor was made of old beams. Jen could peek through the slats into Sunny's stall.

Mrs. DuBois came through the door. Jen couldn't see her but she felt her presence. It chilled Jenny's soul and made the hair on the back of her neck rise up.

"How are my golden horses today?" Mrs. DuBois asked in her sharp voice.

Jen felt the walls quiver every time Sunny crashed into them. She had to clap her hand over her mouth to keep from crying out. Tears flowed freely down her cheeks as she realized the terror Sunny was living under. *She is starving her on purpose. And a colt! Sunny has a colt! How am I going to get them out of here? I'm all alone in this. I can't tell my parents, they don't know I'm here. Daniel can't help, or won't. Tessa? Maybe Tessa can help. I know! I'll call the Humane Society.*

"Come here, Fire. Come and get some sweet feed," commanded Mrs. DuBois roughly. The mare responded by snorting and ducking into the wall. Jenny scooched down lower, wincing in horror at the sickening sounds of Sunny smashing into the wall over and over.

Now I see why she has them in this bank barn. No one can hear anything from the outside. This woman is free to do anything she wants and nobody would know.

"Fine, be that way, no food for you," the woman shrieked, whacking the stall door with her crop. "You'll have to come over here to get anything, you stupid horse. I'll wait. Someday you'll see who is boss. You'll never embarrass me again. Daniel! No grain for the mare. The colt can have a handful," Mrs. DuBois barked over her shoulder as she stormed from the barn.

How could anyone think this is the way to treat a horse? Jen wondered, mystified. *It sounds like she really believes Sunny will obey her. I know that horse. She'll die before she lets that woman near. And that is probably what Mrs. DuBois wants.*

Jenny slithered carefully down the rotten ladder. Daniel stood peering through Sunny's feed slot shaking his head sadly. "She's not going to let my aunt touch her. At least Aunt Vanessa isn't beating her anymore. Her shoulder is starting to bleed. Last time she got really bad before I . . ." He stopped himself, a look of surprise on his face.

"Before you what?" Jenny prompted him.

"Nothin'," he said gruffly. "I didn't do anything."

"We can do something now," she said, tugging at his sleeve. "We can call the animal warden or the police. What's happening here is illegal."

Daniel glared at her. "She's doing what she needs to do to get these horses to obey. She is a famous trainer. She knows what to do."

"Do you really believe that?" Jen whispered, tears welling in her eyes. "Do you believe this is the way you treat anybody? No person or animal should have to go through this. This is *wrong*."

"Well," Daniel huffed, "it must be nice to know everything."

"Daniel," Jen whispered, shocked. "Do *you* think this is the way you train horses?"

"I don't know," he admitted miserably. "Aunt Vanessa promised to help me become a horse trainer if I would work for her here. She told my parents she had some really difficult horses and needed help. That was two years ago. I met Gold N' Fire three months after she had her colt. Aunt Vanessa fed her well while she was pregnant but as soon as we weaned Fire N' Fury the mare returned to her old ways, and she influenced her colt. Now they're both bad. Aunt Vanessa says we have to show them who is boss. What can I do? Without her, I'm homeless."

"You could call the Humane Society or the animal warden." Jenny sniffed again. "You should know that this is wrong."

"I have wondered," he admitted. "I just . . . I can't . . ."

"You mean you won't," Jenny snapped. "Well, maybe I will."

"If you do," Daniel warned, "she'll hide them again. You'll *never* find them. She has friends in high places. She'll know before the animal warden gets here. You might as well say goodbye now. Aunt Vanessa knows everyone."

She ran back to Shannon's car and said nothing to anyone.

🐎   🐎   🐎

Sunny! I've found Sunny! Jenny ran into her house screaming with joy. Nobody answered. She ran from room to room searching. She finally found them outside on the deck. Her folks were talking to someone . . . who was it? Mom, Dad, I've found Sunny.

The adults turned to face her in the same moment. They looked angry . . . and was that other person . . . yes . . . it was Mrs. DuBois. And the police. They were handcuffing her. Taking her away. Tossing her in a cold cell. She heard the cell door slam. It echoed on and on . . . and Mrs. DuBois laughing hysterically.

Jenny sat upright in bed, her heart pounding. It was just a nightmare. It *felt* so real. She glanced at her bedside clock: 3:24 A.M. *Why is this happening to me?* she wondered bitterly.

Chapter Six

"Turn your eyes upon Jesus; look full in His wonderful face, and the things of earth will grow strangely dim, in the light of His glory and grace."

Jen sang the words mechanically. Church just didn't feel comfortable anymore. *The people are the same,* she realized. *It's me. I'm different. I know God exists, I simply don't believe He loves me anymore. If Jesus is so wonderful and so loving, why did He take Sunny away?*

She looked around. Mom and Dad seemed to believe the words of the song. *Why should I want to be with a God who would allow such terrible things to happen to Sunny and me? Why would He want to be with me now? I'm a liar and a sneak. What does He expect? He should know I would try to get her back. This is your fault, God! You have control and this is what You do? It stinks!*

Jenny looked down at her hymnal just as tears began plopping onto the pages. Dad wrapped his brawny arm around her shoulder and pulled her in close to his side. She desperately wanted to stay there, warm and secure, but her anger and guilt surged like a wildfire inside her and she straightened up away from him.

"What's wrong?" Dad mouthed.

She shook her head miserably. "Nothing," she lied. *I can't tell you Dad, you would never understand. I can't tell Tessa because word might get out. She's a blabbermouth. Who can help me . . . Wait! What about Tessa's mom? She's a lawyer. She'll know what to do. That's what I'll do.* She could hardly wait.

"Do you have any proof?" asked Mrs. Silversteen. Her dark eyes, so like Tessa's, searched Jenny's. "Any photos or eye witnesses?"

"Well . . . sort of," Jenny hesitated as she spoke.

"Sort of won't cut it in a court of law." Tessa's mom shook her head. "We need solid evidence. Do you have *any?*"

"There's a groom named Daniel who is helping Mrs. DuBois," Jen replied, "or Aunt Vanessa as he calls her."

"Is she really his aunt?" Mrs. Silversteen leaned forward intently.

"Yes, and he thinks what she is doing is a necessary part of training. He told me that this is part of the breaking process."

"Yes," agreed Tessa's mom thoughtfully. "I think breaking is an appropriate word. She will have many broken things when she's done, including your heart, Jen. Speaking of broken hearts, what do your folks think about this?"

"I . . . I haven't told them," Jenny admitted.

"Don't you suppose that will break your mother's heart?"

Rats! I don't want to think about Mom right now, Jen thought, rolling her eyes.

Tessa's mom shook her head, "Jenny, I can't help you 'til you tell your folks. I'm a lawyer, I know what kind of trouble

I would be in if . . ." her voice trailed off leaving Jen to imagine the different endings to Sunny's fate.

Sunny's only chance is Daniel. I have to convince Daniel to turn in his aunt. And that'll never happen, she thought bitterly.

The phone rang in the Thomas kitchen. "Hello," answered Mom cheerfully. "Hi, Kathy, how are all the O'Rileys? Yes, she's right here. Hold on." Mom handed the phone to Jenny with a severe expression. Jen slapped her forehead. "I totally forgot," she mouthed, shrugging helplessly.

"Hi . . . hi, Kathy," she said.

"Hey, stranger." Kathy's voice sang like always. "How are ya'? We've been praying for you."

Jenny cringed inside. "Thanks, I'm . . . I'm fine."

"Really? You don't sound fine."

"I'm fine," Jen insisted.

"How'd you like to start riding Magnum for me again?" Kathy asked. "I could really use your help. I know you can't jump yet but you could help me condition him."

"Sure," Jen replied. "I'd love that." *Maybe it'll help keep my mind off of Sunny until I can figure out what to do.*

Jen was enveloped in a bear hug. "Oh, I have missed you so much," Kathy exclaimed. "It's been mighty boring around here."

"Can I see Magnum?" Jen asked, feeling strangely shy.

"Right this way, missy."

Some things don't change, Jen thought as she and Magnum floated around the ring. "I had forgotten how nice his trot is," she shouted over her shoulder.

"You guys look awesome!" Kathy yelled back.

Fifteen minutes later Jen was ready to stop. "My legs feel like wet noodles," she complained as she carefully slid down the gelding's side. "I guess I need to work back up to it."

"Yup," Kathy agreed grinning. "Don't worry, a couple days of awful pain and you'll be back, as good as new."

Kathy's comment catapulted Jenny back to her first days at Sonrise Farm; the horse camp where it all started; Magnum's nearly deadly colic . . . all the amazing miraculous things that had happened. *Where are You now God? Have You forgotten Sunny and me?*

Jen's chin began to shake. She tried to undo Magnum's girth, but the pent-up tears made her queasy. She leaned her forehead on the saddle trying to stifle the emotion. Kathy appeared at her side. Jen turned and allowed Kathy to hold her as she sobbed. It seemed like forever before she could stop. Her eyes swelled shut, but her heart felt a little better.

"I don't know how to live without her," Jen said with a hiccup as the older girl led her to a large bale of hay. Jen felt the prickly hay through her britches as they sat.

"I'm so sorry," Kathy replied, shaking her head. "I would pray and ask Him to fill that hole in your heart."

"I don't think so," Jen replied. "I think God is punishing me for something."

Kathy frowned. "Jen, help me put Magnum away, then come with me. I want to show you something." The something was in Kathy's room. Jen was surprised to see how pretty Kathy's room was. The walls were pale blue with a white floral border. White lace curtains and bedspread made it look feminine and fresh. Kathy grabbed her black leather Bible and handed it to Jenny. "Here. Find Romans 8, verse 28."

Jenny fumbled around, then found it.

"Read it," Kathy insisted.

Jen rolled her eyes as she read, "And we know that in all things God works for the good of those who love him, who have been called according to his purpose."

Kathy grabbed Jen's hand, "Jenny, God loves you and He will turn this into good for you."

"I wish I could believe that," Jen whispered. "But I don't. I feel like God has forgotten I even exist. Our pastor was saying I have to give thanks for all things. How can I be thankful that some woman has come to claim Sunny and is now abusing her?"

Whoops, didn't mean to say that, she thought.

Kathy froze. "What? Did you say someone is abusing her?"

Jenny sighed heavily. Her throat felt tight like the tears might start again. "I found Sunny. Mrs. DuBois hates her because Sunny dumped her at a big show years ago. Kathy . . . she thinks that beating and starving horses is how you get them to listen. Daniel says his aunt is a control freak and won't be happy until the mare submits . . . or dies. I've seen her with Sunny. She'll die first."

"Wait, wait, wait . . . slow down. Who's Daniel . . . and you said *horses*. Are there others?"

Jenny explained. "Sunny has a colt. He's maybe three years old. Daniel is Mrs. DuBois's nephew from California.

He's a groom at The DuBois Farm. He did something bad at home and his aunt bailed him out. Kathy . . . she's got the horses hidden in a bank barn surrounded by barbed wire. There's no way to get them out and Daniel won't help. He's afraid to go back home so his aunt's is the only place he has. He told me that if I call the animal warden to turn her in, she'll find out and move them before anyone gets there. I don't know what to do."

Kathy shook her head. "Whew, Jenny this sounds complicated. There *is* a way to recover those horses."

"Really?" Jenny asked hopefully.

"Yeah," Kathy answered. "I'm just not sure what it is."

"Oh." Jenny's shoulders slumped.

"But I do know Someone who does know," Kathy added.

Jen sat up straight again. "Who?"

"The Lord," Kathy said seriously.

"Humph," Jenny grunted.

Kathy stared at her friend. "Jen, you said that your pastor said to give thanks for all things? Are you sure he didn't say 'to give thanks *in* all things'?"

"What's the difference?" Jenny asked grumpily.

"Huge difference," Kathy said. "*In* all things means that even when times are hard—like right now—you can still find *something* to be thankful for."

"Like what?" Jen demanded.

"Like your health, your family, Sunny, for the time you had her and what she meant to you. Especially, Jenny, you should be thankful that you know the Sovereign Lord of the universe, and that He loves you. He already knows how this whole thing will end, and He has it rigged so that it will be for your good. He will take evil and turn it into good. That's what Romans 8:28 means. You can trust Him, Jen, and know that He loves you no matter how *you* feel about Him."

Jen didn't want to hear it. "Whatever," she said.

"Will you do me a *huge* favor?" Kathy asked, batting her eyelashes.

"What?" Jen answered in her annoyed voice.

"Read verses 38 and 39 of Romans 8."

Jenny huffed, then read. " 'For I am convinced that neither death nor life, neither angels nor demons, neither the present nor the future, nor any powers, neither height nor depth, nor anything else in all creation, will be able to separate us from the love of God that is in Christ Jesus our Lord.' That's very nice Kathy. But I still don't *feel* His love right now."

"You know Jen, that's the thing. It's not about a feeling. It's about truth. Truth is truth no matter how you *feel* about it."

"Well, what do I do *now?*" Jenny asked desperately. "I can't leave them there, I can't call anyone, I can't even tell my folks. Dad will forbid me to go back. I'm helping Shannon with her horse and they are coming along really well. I . . . it's driving me crazy!"

"Jenny," Kathy asked, "do you love Sunny?"

"Of course!" Jenny gasped. "How can you even wonder?"

"*Why* do you love Sunny?" Kathy continued.

"I would say because she's mine, but that's not true anymore. So I don't know, I just love her because . . . she's my friend, and I've come to know her, and care for her."

"And does Sunny love you?" Kathy asked.

"I think so, except the last time I saw her she didn't recognize me. Kathy, she didn't even know me!"

"And how did you feel about that?" Kathy asked *very* gently.

"It was terrible! It made me sick inside," Jen cried.

"Why did it make you so sad, Jen?" Kathy probed.

The words rushed out before Jen could even think. "Because . . . I love her and she doesn't trust me anymore!"

"Jenny, are you trusting God? See . . . He loves you even more than you love Sunny. He wants to take care of you even more than you want to take care of Sunny. If you are so busy trying to escape the very One who can help you, you are only harming yourself."

Jen immediately remembered Sunny's bloody shoulder. "Sunny was trying so hard to get away from me, she rubbed her shoulder until it was bleeding."

"Sunny doesn't see you as a friend anymore Jen, and you don't see the Lord as your Friend. But those things aren't truth. Don't believe your circumstances instead of truth, Jen. The Lord is the only One who knows how this will turn out. Your job is only to trust Him. You can do that no matter how you *feel*."

"I still don't get that, Kathy. How can I trust Him if I don't *feel* like I can trust Him?"

"It's simple," Kathy explained. "You talk to Him. It helps me to write to Him. Write a note that says: 'Dear Jesus, I choose to trust You today, no matter how I feel. I trust You to deal with everything, *including* my feelings.' Then, Jenny, just keep talking to Him, even when you're mad. And read your Bible. When you feel doubt, pull out your note and read it. God wants to be with you, the same way you want to be with Sunny. He loves us, so much it makes me cry sometimes. He loves us passionately. He loves us so much, He

sent His Son to die for us. Think about that. That would be like you sending Sunny to die for someone else. It's amazing!"

Lord, asked Jenny, *do You really love me that much?*

More, rang the silent reply, deep in her soul.

"Jenny," Kathy finished, "this is a God-sized problem. *You* can't fix it. Pray about it, ask Him what to do. *And* you need to tell your parents what's going on. The truth *will* come out, so it's much better if it comes from you first."

"Ohhh," Jen groaned, suddenly feeling worse.

"Come on, help me feed the horses and I'll drive you home," said Kathy.

Chapter Seven

Shannon and The Frog trotted smoothly around the ring. Jenny forced herself to focus on the pair. She couldn't stop thinking about the conversation with Kathy.

Shannon guided her mount to the section of fence where Jen perched. "You're not going to disappear on me again are you? You are much nicer than my previous trainer, but I don't like being left alone."

"You weren't alone, Shannon," Jen reminded her. "Tessa was here."

"I know," Shannon said, "but Tessa doesn't know anything about riding. I like my instructor to be with me, you know, instructing."

"Sorry," Jenny replied softly. "I've been a little distracted."

"A little?" Shannon said in a huff.

"OK, a lot distracted," Jen admitted, shrugging. "*Who* was your previous instructor?"

Shannon turned The Frog to answer over her shoulder, "I already told you, silly, Mrs. DuBois. She owns this place you know, and she's a very famous trainer. I was lucky to get private lessons with her. Except that she always yelled at me, and I swear Froggy was petrified of her. She's been too busy lately to teach, and most of her students had to find another trainer." Shannon rode close to Jen. "Actually I'm glad she's not training me anymore. She's scary and loud."

I'll say, Jen thought, watching Froggy walk by. *If you only knew how scary and loud.* But she forced a smile and replied, "I'm really glad I could help you out, Shannon."

Just then, Tessa ran up and thumped Jenny's back *hard.* Jen nearly jumped out of her skin. She turned to say something nasty but stopped as she noticed Tessa's panicked expression. "What?" she asked.

"She's coming!" Tessa squeaked, eyes wide and terrified.

"Who?"

And there she was. Mrs. Vanessa DuBois, climbing out of her navy blue Mercedes, wearing wide jods and shiny black boots. Her blond hair was pulled back in a sleek tight bun with dark sunglasses perched on top of her head. She stalked toward the ring, swinging her crop.

Tessa gasped and ran, grabbing Jenny's shirt to pull her to the nearest cover. The girls slipped behind a boxwood hedge into the barn and found an empty stall with a window to the ring.

Shannon continued riding The Frog, chattering happily to Jen. The Frog saw Mrs. DuBois first. It was the most amazing thing. Jenny had never seen a horse transform so immediately. His walk went from loose and long to short and tight. He suddenly looked like a coiled spring, ready to pop. Shannon twisted in the saddle and gave a little cry.

"Oh! Mrs. DuBois! Umm . . . I thought you were too busy to teach right now."

"No," replied the woman coldly. "I have a little time for you today. I phoned your parents and they said you were here, with some friends. Where are your friends, Shannon?"

Shannon looked around in a panic. "I . . . they were just here. I don't know."

"Shannon, I thought you understood the rules. This is *my* show barn. I do not want your little friends wandering around. Do you understand?"

Tessa glanced at Jenny, then ran out the front of the barn. She headed for the bleachers, stuffing her shirt into her pants as she walked.

"Oh," Shannon gasped, clearly relieved. "H . . . here she is Mrs. DuBois. This is my friend Tessa Silversteen."

Mrs. DuBois stared icily at Tessa. "Are you Shannon's *only* guest? Her parents said she had guestssss."

She sounds like a snake, Jen thought.

"Yes," Tessa lied smoothly. "We dropped a friend off at the skate house on the way. It's just me."

Mrs. DuBois scowled at Tessa, then turned her attention back to the unfortunate Shannon. "Righto," she announced. "Let's begin our lesson, Shannon. We have much to cover today."

Within minutes The Frog began bucking and Shannon was crying as she clung to the pommel of the saddle. Jenny turned her back and slid down the wall until she sat in the fragrant pine shavings. Her heart ached as she listened to Mrs. DuBois screech at Shannon. She grabbed a handful of shavings and scrunched tightly. Then she opened her hand to watch them flutter down softly.

That's what You're doing to me, God, she thought. *You are squeezing me and dropping me onto the ground like sawdust. Do You really love me the way Kathy said?*

More, came the silent reply.

Well, I sure don't feel it, she answered.

Jenny waited there until the lesson ended. It wasn't a long wait. Mrs. DuBois screamed constantly until poor Shannon fell off. "You brainless girl," she heard Mrs. DuBois scream. "You will never be a good rider, and your horse is as stupid as you are!"

Jen rushed from the stall and peered around the corner of the barn. *She's gone!* Shannon sat on the bleacher crying softly. Her white britches were torn and her elbow scraped. Tessa stood nearby holding The Frog's reins loosely. Tessa looked uncomfortable, like she wanted to help but didn't know what to say.

Shannon looked up at Jen with red puffy eyes. "She's right," she cried. "I am a terrible rider. I'll never be any good."

"Don't listen to that woman, Shannon. She's a witch and she doesn't know *anything,*" Jenny exclaimed angrily.

"Who doesn't know anything?" shrieked a voice. Mrs. DuBois swooped from the barn. She stared at Jenny furiously. "Who are you? You look familiar. Well, never mind. Shannon, you have twenty-four hours to remove your horse and belongings. If I *ever* see you or your friends on my property again, I will call the police. Do you understand?" She turned on her heel and strode back to her Mercedes. She glared over her shoulder at Jenny one last time.

Jenny turned her head and knelt down beside Shannon.

Shannon just sat, stunned and pale on the bleacher. "Where will I go?" she mumbled.

Jenny patted Shannon's soft, chubby arm. "Let me call Kathy," she said softly. "I'm sure The Frog can stay at Sonrise Farm for a while."

Shannon nodded gratefully. "I need to call my parents. What do I say? I've never been evicted from a barn before."

Jenny shrugged, "I've never been kicked out of a barn either, so I don't know."

She stood up to sneak a peek at the quarantine barn. The navy Mercedes was parked outside the gate. *Call Kathy, call Kathy. Focus on what you can do right now.*

Kathy answered on the third ring. "Give me an hour," she said. "I'll be there with the trailer. Tell Shannon to call her folks. They need to be there when we move her horse. And Jen, you need to call your folks. I don't want any more trailer accidents!"

Great, thought Jen, *now I'm in for it.*

Mom and Dad arrived, confusion on their faces. Jenny felt ashamed and relieved at the same time. She shrugged her shoulders and ducked her head. "Mom, Dad, I'm sorry."

"Help your friends," Dad said. "We'll talk on the way home."

The Frog climbed eagerly into the trailer, as though he understood they were leaving a terrible place. Jenny slumped in the back seat as they drove through the DuBois Farm's black gate. She turned to gaze out the back window and felt her hope sucked from her like water swirling down the drain. *Oh Sunny! How am I going to watch out for you now? How can I help you if I can't even see you?*

"Jenny, would you like to tell us exactly how you came to be helping Shannon at Mrs. DuBois's farm without telling us?" They were home now and Dad looked really disappointed.

"I didn't think the place was that important?" Jen tried weakly.

"Are you certain it's not because you knew we wouldn't allow it?" He tipped her chin up so she was forced to look into his eyes.

He's crying! she realized.

"Yes," she admitted, "I knew you wouldn't let me go, but Tessa said it wasn't really a lie. I just omitted a detail."

Dad breathed out. "Sweetheart, if something is only partly true, is it true? Truth is truth, complete and whole. Omitting a detail is lying."

"I'm sorry Dad. I just really wanted to see Sunny. More than anything, just *see* her and make sure she was all right." "And did you find her?" Mom asked.

"Yes." Jen nodded and her eyes started to fill up with tears.

"And is she all right?" Dad asked.

"No, she's not! She's being abused by Mrs. DuBois." The words rushed out as she finally told them the whole story.

Dad sat down on the brown sofa next to her. Mom sat on the other side, her fingers stroking Jen's blond hair. Dad scratched his head. "What can we do?"

Mom shook her head. "I don't know. She's on private property."

"I've already talked to Tessa's mom," Jen offered. "She's a lawyer. She said we couldn't do anything without some . . . what was the word—probable cause—or an eyewitness, one who wasn't trespassing. Daniel says we can't call anyone anyway because she would find out and move the horses before anyone got there. Dad, Daniel thinks she may try to kill them. She wants the insurance money."

"Humm," Dad murmured. "We'll have to pray about it, see what He says. In the meantime, we need to talk about your lying to us. I think you shouldn't see Tessa for a while. And I'd like you to talk to Pastor Jeff about it. Not as a punishment—I think you are already feeling punished enough with Sunny. I want you to talk to the pastor because I'm worried about your relationship with the Lord. Deal?"

"Deal," she agreed. "And Dad, I'm really sorry about lying to you and Mom. It made me feel sick to my stomach."

"Good," Dad said. "That was probably the Holy Spirit."

Jenny squirmed in the chair outside Pastor Jeff's office. She was uncomfortable, certain that everyone passing by knew why she was there. She had to spill the whole miserable story again. And it hurt.

"What can I do for you now?" Pastor Jeff asked, once it was out. "You know God has forgiven you, and your folks have forgiven you. Do you have any other questions?"

"Yes," Jen said with a sigh. "Why would God take Sunny from me if He loves me so much?"

"I don't know, Jen," the pastor answered honestly. "I don't believe God *sends* sin into believers' lives. However, thanks to Adam and Eve, sin is present on earth and it always affects others. God gives us free will. He has given Mrs. DuBois free will. God wants us to be close to Him because we *want* to be close. He wants us to obey Him because He knows what is best for us. That means that people can and do choose to go their own way.

"Mrs. DuBois is trying to force Sunny to obey her. She's not worried about Sunny; she wants Sunny to obey because it makes Mrs. DuBois feel better. That's not love—that's control. God *loves* us. He never forces us to love Him back. He knows the only path to peace is His. So, you can choose. I personally have found that life apart from God is no life at all.

"He is the Life, the Way, and the Truth. Him—Jesus. He is your source of everything. And 'if God is for you, Jen, who can be against you?' And He is *for* you."

With those words, Pastor Jeff smiled kindly. Jenny felt her anxiety melting away. But another questions popped out. "When does Mrs. DuBois get to experience the consequences of her own sin?"

"We don't get to know that. That's God's job. Our job is only to trust Him. And then do what He tells us to do. It doesn't always change our circumstances, but it changes everything else. Trusting Him is the only way to peace. It's kind of like Sunny—she is so full of fear, she doesn't even recognize you as a source of help. When we start believing our circumstances or our friends more than the promises or character of God, we do not recognize *our* source of help. You've been locked in a prison of your own making, Jen. I'm so glad you decided to come back." Pastor Jeff hugged her. "I'd like to put you and Sunny on the prayer chain if that's OK with you."

"Sure," Jen shrugged. "It can't hurt."

"And can we pray now?" he asked.

"Yes."

"Oh, Jesus," Pastor Jeff said, "thank You for loving us so much, even when we're lost and confused. Thanks for forgiving us and for becoming our very source of life. Protect Sunny and I ask that You help Jenny to forgive Mrs. DuBois. Thank You again, that You already know how this will end, and that You are here for Jenny."

"Amen," they said together.

Jenny smiled. "Thanks, Pastor Jeff. I really do feel better."

"See you at church," he called, crinkling his blue eyes as she walked out.

"How did it go?" Mom asked as they walked toward the parking lot.

"He's really nice," Jenny admitted. "I was a little scared, but we talked about cool things."

"Like what?" Mom asked as she opened the car door.

"Like . . ." Jen ducked inside the station wagon before continuing. "Like, God loving *me* the way I love Sunny. I never could get my mind around it till now. Mom, I really thought *God* did all this to me to punish me for *something*."

"Suffering is hard to understand, Jenny. Especially when someone you love is suffering and you can't do anything about it. I think that's the hardest."

"So what do we do now?" asked Jenny. "About Sunny. I don't feel like I can leave her there, but I don't see anything else I can do. Without Daniel's help, I'm helpless."

"Now Jenny, that is just not true. If God is for you, and we know He is, who can be against you? Some people think prayer is the last resort. Well, it's my first defense. It is the best weapon against evil. You and I will pray for Sunny, constantly. We can pray while we're driving, eating, mucking stalls, or showering. Deal?"

"Deal!" Jen agreed.

"Dad will want to join us. We'll tell him when we get home."

Chapter Eight

It was in the *Washington Herald*. A huge ad—The Washington Horse Expo—thousands of demonstrators and vendors. Jen could see the ad from across the table. "Dad, may I see that section of the newspaper when you're finished?"

He folded the paper back into neat quarters. "Sure," he said with a smile. "Here ya' go."

She laid it out flat on the floor and gazed at it. The phone rang. Dad grabbed it. "Hold on, Kathy. She's right here." He handed Jenny the phone.

"Hey, Kathy," Jen began.

"Jen," Kathy interrupted. "The Washington Horse Expo is here! I'm going tomorrow morning. You wanna' join me? I'll buy you lunch, especially if you'll help me feed and muck before."

"Let me ask." She covered the mouth piece with her hand, "Dad, can I go to the Horse Expo with Kathy tomorrow?"

"Sure," he smiled peeking over the top of the classified section.

"He said Yes," she reported happily. "It's weird, I was just looking at the ad myself."

"Great minds think alike," Kathy said cheerfully. "I'll pick you up tomorrow morning around 7:00."

"See ya' then," Jen agreed.

The expo was packed. Jenny and Kathy felt squeezed like a tube of toothpaste as they followed the crowd through the turnstile. A frazzled sweaty young man stamped the backs of their hands as they slipped past. Jenny gazed at the purple stamp as it dried.

"Come on," Kathy shouted above the noise, "let's grab a program. Do you want to get a lemonade?"

Jenny shook her head. "I'm fine right now. Let's go see some horses."

Kathy nodded agreement and they headed toward the exhibition hall. Along the way, Kathy stared at the program she had picked up. "Who should we see? There are a bunch of trainers here. Look, here's that guy who works with wild horses. Colton Wright. Let's go see him. He's doing a demonstration in fifteen minutes."

The girls made their way through the crowd. It was standing room only at the round pen where the demo was to take place. Jen tried everything to get a good view. *It's no fun being short,* she decided. She craned her neck around to see up into the bleachers. *Is there any space up there?* she wondered. *I would even sit in the nosebleed section if I could see something. Way up there . . . is that . . . Daniel? What is he doing here? What if Mrs. DuBois is here too?* She jerked around back quickly, hoping he hadn't seen her.

"Hey little lady," said a familiar voice behind her.

Jen turned slightly. There stood Dr. Davis, the Sonrise

Farm veterinarian. "Dr. Dave," she shrieked, thrilled. "How are you?"

Kathy turned around. "Hey, Doc. What are you doing here?"

The wiry vet grinned; he held popcorn in one hand, soda in the other. "This guy says he can fix any behavior problems a horse might have. I want to see for myself. Do you girls need a spot to sit?"

"Sure," they said in harmony.

They followed him up three rows where he kicked out two of his vet-tech helpers. "You guys go find new seats—these ladies need yours," he growled good-naturedly. The young men grinned at Kathy and Jen as they squeezed past.

Perfect, she thought, settling in. *Not too high and I can see over everyone's heads.*

A huge copper chestnut stallion bolted through the gate of the metal round pen, squealing and snorting as it crashed shut behind him. He galloped, bucking around the pen. He stopped suddenly, head up, and stared at the gate. He blew loudly through his nostrils, then shied violently as Mr. Wright walked toward the gate.

The trainer fiddled with his headset, adjusting the microphone. He was not a small man, though he looked small compared to the massive horse in the round pen. The stallion shook his head threateningly as he trotted toward Mr. Wright.

"Good morning, fellow horse lovers. My name is Colton Wright." He shook his rope at the horse to move him away. "And I have discovered something amazing about horses. They have a nonverbal language of their own, and I can speak it. I can show you how to do the same.

"This horse is a Dutch Warmblood stallion. His name is Gradiff. He's eleven years old and has become increasingly difficult to handle. His new owners are allowing me to use him in the demonstration today because conventional methods have failed. This horse has been started, ridden, and shown. He was mishandled for a period of time and is now, well, I would have to call him dangerous. The alternative for this stallion is to be put down—euthanasia."

Jenny leaned forward on the bleacher spellbound as Colton Wright moved the horse around the round pen. The trainer used nothing but the white rope. He flung it toward the horse's hindquarters to keep him moving. The big stallion galloped around at first then cantered around for what seemed like hours.

Colton Wright kept up a monologue describing each step as it occurred. "You see, horses and humans are natural enemies. Humans are predators, horses are prey. No matter how much we love our horses, they are always waiting for the inevitable. They know that many of us had meat for lunch, and horses are made of meat. For the horse, instinct says 'run first, ask questions later.' It would be sort of like you living with a bunch of lions, would you ever really feel safe?

"What happens in your barn when your horse rears or pulls away from you? Do you yell at him? Do you slap him? Do you whip him? All those responses make his fear and flight response *stronger*. So next time you place him in that situation, he'll make sure he gets away from you.

"Folks, if you want your horse to love you, *you* need to be a place of safety and comfort. I am treating this stallion the way his mama did when he was a colt. I will work with nature and instinct instead of against it. I am pushing him away from me using the rope and my eyes. I am square and all my movements are square. I face him with my eyes on his eyes. I don't want to hit him with the rope. I simply use it as a visual stimulus to keep him moving.

"Right now, for Gradiff, running around is comfort. He wants to get away from me. In just a little while, he'll come to the end of his natural resources, or his biological flight distance, and the movement will stop being a source of comfort. In other words, he will get tired. Then he'll need to reach for some sort of agreement with me. Until then I'll keep him moving, not hurting or scaring him. I will allow *him* to make the decision. The first sign we will have that he is beginning to think about me is his inside ear. He will turn it toward me, and keep it on me."

Jenny watched as the horse slowed slightly. The stallion's eyes still blazed with fury but he wasn't pounding the ground as hard when he ran. Then, almost on cue, the stallion turned his inside ear in toward Mr. Wright.

"All right, now I have his attention. I am going to begin asking him to change directions. In the horse world, the one who controls the direction gets to be boss. I am going to raise my rope and step toward his head. I don't want to get too close and I do not want to invite him into *my* space. I have had many stallions get in my space with their mouths open, hoping to have my head as a snack. Now what I'm looking for is some licking and chewing from Mr. Gradiff. This will let me know that he's thinking about what I'm saying, chewing on it, shall we say."

Again, as though Mr. Wright had read Gradiff's mind, the big stallion began to lick his lips, his pace slowing to a trot. *Whew is he gorgeous,* thought Jen.

77

"The final signal I'm looking for is for this horse to put his head down, as he is trotting around. It will almost look as though he is trying to eat off the ground. This means that he is offering to negotiate and he'll let me lead the meeting."

The coppery stallion dropped his head to the ground. It did indeed look as though he was trying to eat while trotting.

Jen couldn't move. Her heart pounded in her ears as she listened to Mr. Wright.

"Now," he whispered into his headset. "I move my eyes from his eyes back down to his withers, then to the ground. I need to watch him carefully because he is a stallion. I turn my body and round my shoulders. I will continue to watch him from the corner of my eye."

The stallion stopped trotting and came in almost immediately. He came within inches of Mr. Wright's head. He stood, muscles quivering, waiting, The trainer reached out carefully and stroked the big forehead. Gradiff licked his lips and blew out in relief.

Mr. Wright walked and Gradiff followed him peacefully. The audience burst into applause. The din caused Gradiff to tuck his tail and lunge forward. Mr. Wright just reached up to stroke the chestnut neck and the horse stopped. He gazed at Mr. Wright as if to say, "What was that?"

"Oh, that's just people clapping for you," answered Mr. Wright into his mike.

The demonstration ended with Mr. Wright rubbing Gradiff all over. The massive stallion's eyes were soft; his head low and relaxed. He did not look like the same horse. *If I hadn't seen that with my own eyes, I would not believe it,* Jen thought to herself once she could breathe.

"And that is a small taste of my Trusting-Bond method," Mr. Wright announced as he and Gradiff left the round pen together. "I will be in my booth later, number 589, if any of you have questions. Thank you, you've been a great crowd." And he disappeared into the back with Gradiff following closely.

Jenny glanced at Kathy. Tears ran down the older girl's face. Jenny felt unable to move. She was elated, weepy, awestruck, just downright confused. *Was that real?* she wondered. The girls sat waiting together as the crowd herded down the steps. Jen happened to look up to notice Daniel still sitting, head in his hands. *Is he crying?* she wondered. She realized she was staring and looked away.

"That was the most amazing thing I have ever seen," Kathy finally whispered.

"Do you think we could go talk to him?" Jen begged.

Kathy nodded. "Absolutely. He said he was in booth 589, right? Let's go now."

They waded through the crowd. Kathy turned to Jen, "I can't imagine what this place will be like this weekend. It's going to be a zoo!" Jen nodded and grabbed Kathy's shirt to keep from losing her. Booth 589 was swarming with bodies. Jen couldn't even *see* Mr. Wright.

"OK, let's go to plan B," Kathy shouted. "Let's grab some lunch and come back later."

Kathy headed to the ladies room while Jen saved a place in line for lunch. Her thoughts whirled making her almost dizzy. *Sunny! Mr. Wright could help with Sunny! But how?*

Daniel walked by, head high, smiling joyfully. He looked up and caught her eye just as they both heard the shrill, harsh voice of Vanessa DuBois. Jenny turned away and was able to shield most of herself behind a large man in line.

"Did you see that, Aunt Vanessa?" she overheard Daniel say excitedly.

"See what?" she asked. "That trainer? I've seen him before. Those horses are drugged. I hope you didn't fall for that 'natural' mumbo jumbo, Daniel. Don't be so gullible. Nope . . . showing them who's boss is the only way."

"What about Fire?" he questioned quietly. "Why isn't it working with her and her colt?"

"Stop it," she hissed, looking around furtively. "Don't talk about this here, you fool! And the reason it doesn't work with her is because she is too stupid and stubborn—kind of like you!"

Daniel dropped his eyes. It was as if someone had drained all the life and joy from him. Jen suddenly understood why Daniel couldn't or wouldn't help her. He was as terrified of his aunt as Sunny was.

Jenny watched them walk away, a lone tear trailing down her cheek.

Her watch said 1:30. "Let's go back," she begged.

Kathy nodded and sucked on her straw until it made empty slurpy noises. "OK, all done." The girls threw their trash in the big metal can and headed quickly back to Booth 589. "It looks like the crowd is breaking," Kathy hollered above the noise.

Yeah, said Jenny to herself. *At last.*

Then they saw why the crowd was breaking. Jen's excitement dissolved into frustration. He was gone! Jenny looked desperately around but he was truly gone.

"I guess everyone needs to eat," Kathy said with her smile. "It's all right Jen, we'll see him. Let's go look at the other booths for now."

But to Jenny, the Expo had lost its appeal. *All I want to do is talk to Mr. Wright,* she thought. *I don't want to look at new fly sprays or dewormers. I want to see if Trust-Bonding would work with Sunny!*

And then there he was. Colton Wright, looking at the new fly sprays. Jenny went near, but couldn't think of how to begin the conversation. Mr. Wright fingered the corner of a flysheet, then headed off in the direction of the food court.

Jenny followed. *I feel like I'm stalking him,* she realized.

Mr. Wright suddenly turned around to stare directly at her. His faded blue eyes were kind but intense. Jenny returned his gaze, unable to speak. "Can I help you young lady?" he asked kindly. He pulled off his wide-brimmed hat and ran his hand through his gray hair.

Jen dissolved into tears. "I have a horse, I mean I had a horse . . . she's being abused and starved and I can't tell anyone," she sobbed. *Please say you'll help me. Please.*

Mr. Wright waited patiently.

The whole story tumbled from Jen's lips, uncontrolled. Mr. Wright never appeared surprised or upset. By the time she finished, she could almost breathe again. *Please help.* Her heart seemed to beg all on it's own. Only all it could say was *please.*

"So," he spoke in almost a whisper. "Sunny is still in a bad place and you want to help her, is that what you're saying?"

"Yes," she sniffled. "Can you ... will you help?"

"Jenny," the older man said as he shook his head, "as much as I want to help, Sunny is not yours. I can't do anything with a horse without permission from the owner. Do you think Mrs. DuBois would bring Sunny to a demo or allow me to come to her place?"

"You don't understand—Mrs. DuBois is the one hurting Sunny."

"Jenny," the trainer said softly, "this is one tough situation. If I can ever help you with a horse that *belongs* to you, I will. Here is my card. I will pray for you and Sunny too." And he patted her back gently, then walked away.

Jen leaned on a barrel feeling numb. *OK Lord, I'm praying for Sunny. I really thought Mr. Wright was going to help. Tell me what to do!*

Trust Me.

Kathy ran around the corner. "Jenny! Where have you been? You scared me."

Jen shook her head. "He won't help. He says I need to pray."

"Oh," Kathy said, understanding. "I didn't realize Mr. Wright was a believer."

"Can we go home now," Jen pleaded. She felt exhausted beyond belief.

"Sure," Kathy replied. "I'm sorry, Jenny. I know you're disappointed. The Expo is here for four days if you want to come back."

Jen couldn't answer.

Chapter Nine

Shannon arrived at Sonrise Farm shortly after Kathy and Jen returned. She walked into the paddock and retrieved The Frog. "Jenny," she shouted, "will you help me with him?"

"I don't really feel like it today, Shannon," Jen called back.

"Oh," Shannon answered dejectedly.

Jenny walked to the fence rail and hung her arm over the top rail. She played with The Frog's velvety nose.

"You could show me around the farm," Shannon suggested hopefully.

It would be sort of like my first tour around Sonrise Farm, Jen thought, remembering that amazing day. It was when Kathy had mentioned that she was a believer. *It was the beginning of the happiest days of my life,* Jenny realized. *Would taking Shannon make me feel better or worse?*

Jen glanced at Shannon who had the nerve to be giving *Jenny* the sad puppy look.

"Cut it out, Shannon," she giggled. I'm already familiar with that look. All right, I'll take you on a tour of Sonrise Farm. Let me go ask Kathy who I should ride. Saddle up your steed. I'll be right back."

Jen headed for the house suddenly aware of the amazing situation she was in. *Here I am, friends with the owner of a horse farm, being begged to help other people with their horses. Several horses to ride at any time. Last year I would have given anything I owned to be able to be here.* It stopped her in her tracks. She drew in a huge lung filling breath. *Lord,* she said, her spirit reaching out for Him. *Please forgive me. I am thankful for Sonrise Farm and Kathy.*

Kathy looked up from her magazine on the kitchen table when she heard the screen door slam.

"Hey, Jen, are you all right? You want a glass of water?"

"Sure, I can get it," Jen waved Kathy back down. "Shannon wants a tour of the farm. Is that OK? Who should I ride?" Jenny waited for an answer while she filled her glass. There was no response. She turned back around to see Kathy smiling hugely.

"What?" she asked taking a big glug of water. "What's so funny?"

"You're back." Kathy kept smiling.

Jen snorted. "What do you mean?"

Kathy shrugged. "I don't know, you just suddenly seem more like your old self. It's neat. Oh . . . who should you take? Mmm, take Chance. He's been sitting for a week. He could use a little hack. Hey, there's a new filly in the broodmare barn, born last week."

Jen gasped. "Why didn't you tell me?"

Kathy looked surprised, " I don't know, it just didn't seem as important as . . . you know, Sunny. Anyway, go look at her. She's adorable. And have fun."

It is just like old times, Jen thought as she tacked up the old chestnut school horse.

Shannon and The Frog seemed to do just fine together. The summer sun made both horses quiet and sleepy. It was wonderful to be back in the saddle, just pooping around. The filly was absolutely adorable. Her tiny hooves and fuzzy mane shot Jen back to this exact time and place last year. "Thank You, Lord," she said aloud.

"What was that?" Shannon asked.

Jenny smiled. "I was just thanking the Lord for this filly, and for this whole place, and for my whole life." Things inside were breaking loose. Jenny could feel joy welling up as she thanked Him. Her eyes filled. It was overwhelming.

Shannon stared at Jen doubtfully, as though perhaps she had lost her mind. Jen smiled kindly at the other girl. "Come on, let me show you the other broodmares."

They had a lovely tour and Shannon even sat through The Frog spooking at a bird. "Wow," Shannon crowed, "that's the first time I've stayed on when he shied!"

Jenny saw Shannon through new eyes. "How many times have you fallen off this horse?"

Shannon blushed deeply. "I don't know, more times than I can count." She shook her head as she said it. "That's why Mrs. DuBois said I would never be a good rider."

"Well, Mrs. DuBois is wrong," Jenny said firmly. "I think the first thing we need to do is find you a quieter horse to learn on."

"Sell The Frog?" Shannon screeched. "Nope, won't do it." She leaned down to wrap her arms around the chestnut neck.

"No, silly. I would just put you on one of the school horses until you could get some basic skills. Part of your problem right now is that you are so concerned with stopping and turning this big guy you can't really focus on you. Let's ask Kathy who you can ride."

"OK," Shannon agreed happily.

"You know, we should get a booth here next year," Kathy said on day two of the Expo. "It snuck up on me this year, but it would be great marketing for our jumpers."

"I could help you," Jen suggested.

"OK!" Kathy agreed. "We'll pick up the information for that today."

"It seems quieter," Jenny mused, looking around.

"Well, it's day two," Kathy explained. "The excitement has worn off a little and it's not the weekend yet. Friday is usually quiet, relatively speaking of course. What would you like to see today?"

Jen flipped through her program. She found the name and list of times. "Can we go listen to Colton Wright again?" she asked.

Kathy flipped to the correct day in her program. "He's lecturing, it's not a demo. It would be in room 12 on the west side. Let's go!"

The room was packed; there were seats scattered sparsely, but no two together.

"We'll have to sit apart," Kathy said loudly. "There's a spot down there. I'll sit here."

Jenny apologized as she squished her way down the packed aisle to the vacant seat.

Colton Wright walked out. His entrance drew a burst of applause. "Thank you, thank you, ladies and gents," he grinned. "I am honored to be here at the Washington Horse

Expo. My Trust-Bonding method is beginning to catch on in this part of the country. My goal in life is to have every horseman, woman, and child have the kind of relationship with their horses that I have with mine. I love to teach folks how to have a relationship with their horse. Not just be the automatic feeder that shows up twice a day, but to have your horse really want to be with you. How many of you would like that?"

Dozens of hands flew up.

Jenny listened as Mr. Wright told stories of how he had developed his Trust-Bonding method. It made so much sense. He finished the lecture by asking, "So how many of you out there would like to learn how to do what I do the Wright Way?"

He threw a couple of beach balls into the crowd, "See how long you guys can keep these up in the air. He threw in two more. Jenny grew dizzy watching for them. Mr. Wright added some music. "All right, when the music stops, the balls stop."

The music stopped. The ball landed in Jen's lap. She blinked once, then grabbed it.

"Who has a ball?" Mr. Wright asked.

Jen and three others stood.

"Who has a ball that says, 'The Wright Way?' "

The sandy-haired young man in the corner with the horn-rimmed glasses raised his hand.

"You get my complete pack of tools," announced Mr. Wright handing the young man a bag. "It comes with a halter, lead rope, long-stick, video, and instruction book. What's your name, son?"

The young man pushed his glasses back up on his nose and cleared his throat. "My name is Tim."

"Well, Tim, do you have any horses?" Mr. Wright asked as he placed the videotape onto the tower of items in Tim's arms.

"No, but my girlfriend does. She has two," Tim answered, trying to balance the video with his chin.

"I guess we know who's getting your prize," laughed Mr. Wright, waving to the dark beauty sitting next to Tim. "And let's see, whose ball says . . . books?"

Two people rose.

"You both get my complete training manual." Mr. Wright tossed each of them a thick paperback. "There are coupons in there also for discounts on my other stuff. Enjoy."

Jenny was beginning to feel disappointed. She looked on her ball, there were no words, just four little rectangles drawn on it. What could this be? she asked herself. All the good prizes have been won. I would have loved that complete training packet, or even the manual.

"And for my final prize today . . . whose ball has four boxes on it?"

Jen rose.

Mr. Wright walked over. "Hi again, young lady," he smiled kindly. "You have just won tickets for four people to come to my farm in Pennsylvania for a week."

Jenny plopped down abruptly. Breathe, breathe.

Mr. Wright helped her to her feet. He kept his arm under hers. "I met this young lady yesterday so I already know her deal. Bring your parents and brother or sister or whoever. We'll have a wonderful time!" He jogged back up to the podium. "Thank you all for coming, and don't miss my demo at 3:30 today. I'll be putting a saddle on Gradiff."

The crowd dispersed through the double doors. Jenny sat in her metal folding chair opening and closing her mouth. She felt like a fish, but she couldn't help it. No words would come out.

Kathy ran over and sat next to her. "Congrats," she said, grinning. "We should probably phone your folks."

Mr. Wright approached. "Here are the tickets. Let my manager know which week works for you. You can choose to watch me train young or troubled horses, or we can all just ride my wonderful trail horses. You can also schedule yourselves for a clinic, but they all have very limited openings, so check with Joe on that. I look forward to meeting your parents, young lady." The trainer doffed his cowboy hat and winked at Jen.

"Wow," breathed Jenny. "I . . . I don't know what to say."

"How 'bout, 'Thanks, Lord,' " Kathy suggested.

"Thanks, Lord!" Jen repeated breathlessly.

Jen enjoyed watching her mom gasp and gulp like a fish too.

"Kathy, did you meet this man? How do we know this is, you know . . . safe?"

"Well," Kathy replied. "He is one of the best-known trainers on the East Coast. He has a Web site. It's www.TheWrightWay dot something. Let's check it out. You can also call his general manager. Jen and I saw Mr. Wright do amazing things with an abused and vicious stallion. Plus," Kathy added with a mischievous grin, "I could go with you guys, strictly as a service to you, with no thought for myself." She burst out laughing. "It would be a blast!"

They called Joe, the general manager and signed all four of them up for a week of trail riding. They would leave in two weeks.

"I've never ridden a horse," Dad said a little nervously. "Do you think he'll have nice ones?"

"I'll teach you how to ride Daddy," Jen said as she hugged him. "Plus, I think Mr. Wright rides western. We'll find a big ol' quarter horse for you. Maybe we could give you some lessons before we leave. Kathy?"

"Sure," Kathy replied. "You can ride one of my dad's heavy hunters. We'll put on a lunge line and teach you the basics. Great idea, Jen."

"What about me?" Jen's mom asked mournfully.

"Sorry, Mrs. Thomas," laughed Kathy. "Didn't mean to leave you out. We'll do a Thomas family group lesson."

Jenny lay in bed that night confused and excited. "Lord," she whispered. "I still don't understand why You let Sunny get taken away. I choose to trust You, even if I don't feel like I trust You."

If God is for you, who can be against you?

"I guess that's my problem Lord, are You for me or against me?"

Jenny suddenly remembered reading Kathy's Bible. She grabbed hers from her bedside table. *What verse was that?* "Something in Romans." She flipped to the back of the Book. "Romans 8:28." She repeated it over and over to keep it fresh while she searched. "8:28, 8:28. There it is.

'And we know that in all things God works for the good of those who love him, who have been called according to his purpose.'" *What does that mean, Lord, right now?*

It means, Jen, that I know all things and I will work them out for your good.

"What about Sunny?" she whispered into the darkness.

Especially Sunny, He promised.

She read on to find verses 38 and 39: "For I am convinced that neither death nor life, neither angels nor demons, neither the present nor the future, nor any powers, neither height nor depth, nor anything else in all creation, will be able to separate us from the love of God that is in Christ Jesus our Lord."

"If you love me so much Lord, why did You take my horse away?"

Because she wasn't your horse.

"What do I need to do now, Lord?" Jen asked.

Trust Me. Keep your eyes on Me.

I will, she promised. And she wrote Him a note saying so.

Chapter Ten

Mom drove Jen to Sonrise Farm to help Kathy with the mucking. Shannon's driver pulled in right behind them. Shannon fell out of the Jaguar and rushed toward Jen, almost stepping on her toes. Jen backed up to protect her feet.

"Jenny! Jenny, look what I found at the tack shop," Shannon shrieked. "It's a show, one I can do with Froggy."

"You guys aren't ready for a show," Jen answered with a snort.

"It's just a *little* show," Shannon tried to explain. "I really want to do it, but I need your help."

Jen shook her head. "I don't know, Shannon."

"I'll help you, Shannon," Kathy said.

Jenny spun around. "Hey, how long have you been eavesdropping?"

"Long enough to hear your friend asking for help. You guys have been working for three weeks now. Give poor Chance a break. I'll trailer you, if you want, Shannon."

Shannon eagerly pulled out the program. "See here, Novice Equitation. No jumping, just walk, trot, canter. I can do that. Just one class? It's two weeks away."

Jenny looked closely. "No, Shannon, look at the date. That's the day we're supposed to leave for Mr. Wright's farm. And it's a five hour drive to Pennsylvania."

"Oh." Shannon's face dropped.

Kathy looked at the program for a moment. "Her class is at 11:00. We would be back here by 1:00 at the latest. We weren't planning to leave until 3:00 anyway. We could fit it all in."

"All right," Jen agreed, rolling her eyes. "It seems like a lot of trouble for one class."

"Jen," Kathy whispered. "Encourage her. She's your only student."

Jenny caved in. "Alright, if Kathy will drive, I guess we have to!"

Jenny spent most of her time at Sonrise Farm with Shannon and Kathy getting Shannon ready for the show. They used Chance as a lesson horse for the first week, then Shannon gained enough confidence to ride her own horse again. Jenny continued working Magnum and when she felt herself doubting God's goodness, she pulled out her worn, crumpled note. She had begun writing verses on it too. Like Jeremiah 29:11: " 'For I know the plans I have for you, ... plans to prosper you and not to harm you.' " She said them out loud often. *It's not that it hurts less, Lord, it's just that I have no option. I will choose to trust You because otherwise I'll go crazy.*

You can trust Me, Jenny.

She really didn't want to see all the familiar faces from

the show circuit. They would want to know what had happened, how, why . . . *it would be much easier to simply stay away. On the other hand, I remember what it was like to do my first show. Why does it have to be so hard, Lord? Sunny and I should be doing this together.*

Trust Me—the thought kept prickling her. **Trust Me. I know the plans I have for you,... plans to prosper you and not to harm you.**

The Frog didn't want to load. He reared and balked as he approached the trailer. Jenny felt her patience wearing thin. "Maybe we're not meant to go to this show, Shannon," she suggested hopefully.

"We'll manage," Kathy insisted, coaxing the Thoroughbred closer.

"I have some treats," piped Shannon.

"We don't want to use treats," Kathy replied. "We want him to decide to get on the trailer." She pulled the restless horse to the ramp, then backed him up. He came a little closer the second time and Kathy let him. Then she backed him again.

"Hey, you're going the wrong way," Jen called.

"It's reverse psychology," Kathy explained. "It will make him want to go forward into the trailer."

"Hmm," Jen huffed.

Three attempts and it worked! The Frog climbed right in.

"Wow," said Shannon. "How did you do that?"

"I don't know," Kathy said with a shrug. "Hop in, we're late."

They arrived late. Jen tacked up Froggy while Kathy helped Shannon register.

Shannon did amazingly well, staying calm as her mount jigged and shied at every little thing. Jenny led The Frog into the lower ring to help Shannon warm up.

"Breathe, Shannon. And relax your shoulders. You're as stiff as dry spaghetti. Remember to shrug your shoulders. Think about lying on a beach. Oh, look at that, now he's relaxing too."

Shannon's smile was brilliant. Her plump, shiny face beamed with excitement.

"Jen, I've only got five minutes before my class. What should I do?" "Yawn, Shannon. Big yawn."

"What?"

"Just try it," Jen insisted.

Shannon yawned and Jen opened her mouth to yawn and stretch. "Oh, I'm so sleepy," she said playfully.

The effect on Shannon's mount was amazing. His head dropped, his eyelids drooped and he looked ready to fall asleep right there on deck for their class.

Shannon stared at Jen. "How . . . oh, never mind, I'm up next. Jenny, are my parents here yet?"

Jen scanned the parking lot. "I see their car, but not them. They're probably inside waiting for you guys."

The crackly loudspeaker announced the beginning of the Novice Equitation class.

"Wish me luck," yelled Shannon over her shoulder."

"I don't believe in luck," Jenny called back, cupping her hand around her mouth.

"Keep them safe, Lord," she whispered as she walked to the rail of the big indoor arena. There were ten horses in Shannon's class. Half were young Thoroughbreds like The Frog, half were ponies.

"Take the rail to the right at a walk. Please walk to the right," the judge requested. Shannon pulled smoothly on her right rein guiding Froggy to the rail of the show ring.

Jen looked around the indoor bleachers as her eyes grew accustomed to the darkness. She nudged Kathy with her elbow. "There are Shannon's parents."

"Oh good," Kathy replied without looking.

"Trot, please, everyone trot."

All the riders urged their mounts into a trot and began posting. Shannon appeared relaxed and smiling. The Frog was going along very nicely.

"Walk please, everyone walk."

Shannon sat deep and stopped posting, The Frog transitioned down smoothly.

Jenny grinned, "I guess I am a good instructor."

Kathy shot her a playful look. "Only as good as *your* instructor."

"Canter please, everyone canter," the judge requested.

The Frog was a little bumpy to begin with, but Shannon sat deep and they smoothed out. The gray mare in front of Shannon's horse picked up the wrong lead and her rider snatched the reins to correct her. The gray jerked to a trot and The Frog got a little too close. The mare pinned her ears, wringing her tail in warning.

"Ooh, what a nasty mare," Kathy exclaimed. "Shannon better stay far away from her hind end, or Frog will get kicked in the teeth."

Shannon quickly guided Froggy in a small circle toward the center of the ring and away from the ill-tempered mare. They made their way back to the rail and continued smoothly.

"Well done, Shannon," Kathy whispered, clapping silently.

Yeah, Shannon, Jenny thought, remembering the day they were evicted from The DuBois Farm.

"Hey, Jennifer Thomas! What are you doing here?" called a loud voice from outside the arena.

"Sshhh," Jen hissed turning around.

It was Linda Hill, one of Jenny's former competitors. "You're not showing today, are you?" asked Linda fearfully.

"No, I'm not. I'm watching a friend," Jen answered, turning back around. *I hope that gets rid of her* she thought. *I do not need to be talking to Linda Hill right now.*

No such luck.

"Hey," Linda continued, "wasn't that your mare I saw on the news a while back? Something about her being stolen or something?"

"Yes, that was Sunny and yes she was stolen and yes she has been found by her original owner." Jen growled. *Surely that will make her go away.*

Didn't work.

"Well, how was she stolen? Wasn't she a rare Palomino Thoroughbred and really valuable?" Linda was closing in for the kill, clearly enjoying herself.

Kathy stepped in. "Hi, Linda, we have a new student we're watching so we really can't talk just now. We'll see you after the class if you want." She said it firmly and kindly. Linda pulled herself away in a huff.

"Thanks," Jen whispered, dangerously close to losing it.

Kathy smiled warmly at her. "I'm proud of you, Jen. I know this is hard. This place has so many memories for both of us. It's good of you to help your friend. I'll keep the vultures at bay, you focus on Shannon. I think she'll place."

Their eyes went back to Shannon. *One more downward transition in this direction,* Jen thought.

"Walk please, everyone walk."

Shannon and The Frog did it perfectly. They slowed gently and smoothly. The nasty gray mare lashed out at a pony following too closely. One of the other Thoroughbreds crow-hopped.

"Halt please, everyone halt. Reverse and walk."

The class was put through their paces to the left. Shannon and her horse did everything without a misstep.

"Walk and line up," came the final instructions. "Walk please and line up."

The group slowed to walk then came into the center and stood. Frog jigged in place, just a little. Shannon glanced at Jenny. Jen yawned widely. Shannon sucked in a deep breath and blew out. The Frog relaxed visibly.

The judge called the third place winner. "Mary Sanders on Pennywhistle, from Windamere Farms. And the second place winner is . . . Robin Casey on Blue Max, from The DuBois Farm."

Jenny and Kathy stared at each other. *DuBois Farm!* Jenny caught Shannon's eye. Shannon looked surprised but didn't move in her saddle.

"And the blue ribbon goes to Shannon Lockhart on The Frog, from Sonrise Farm!"

Shannon urged The Frog toward the judge. The big horse stood quietly while the judge pinned the blue ribbon on his bridle. Shannon beamed as though she had won Olympic gold. She walked the gelding out of the ring, hopped off, and threw her arms around Jenny's neck. "We did it," she puffed excitedly. "You were right, Jenny. I'm not a terrible rider. Thank you."

Jenny glimpsed the angry face of Mrs. DuBois out of the corner of her eye. *I feel sorry for poor Robin,* she thought. *She's gonna get it for losing to Shannon.*

Jen was right. They walked past Mrs. DuBois scolding Robin for messing up.

The woman glanced up as they walked past. "You," she screeched. "You there with Shannon. What is your name?"

Jenny glanced at Kathy. "What should I do?" she mouthed silently.

"Keep walking," Kathy answered out loud. They walked quickly toward the trailer.

"Let's load him up and get out of here," Kathy whispered leaning forward to talk around The Frog.

Mrs. DuBois abandoned her student and came after them.

Kathy was motioning Jenny and Shannon on. "Mrs. DuBois, these are my students. Please leave them alone."

"I knew I recognized you from somewhere. You are the ones who stole my horse," she screamed after them. "I know who you are. And you," she pointed a long red fingernail directly at Jen. "I found you trespassing and snooping around my barn. You're the one who made me evict Shannon." Mrs. DuBois squinted angrily at Jenny. "You'll never see that wretched mare again. I'll see to that." She turned abruptly on her heel and strode away.

"*That* is one angry woman," breathed Kathy. "OK, let's take a deep breath and finish up here. Congratulations Shannon. You rode very well.

"Thanks," Shannon answered. "It was really fun. And thank you, Jenny. I couldn't have done that without you."

"You're welcome," Jenny said sincerely. Then she turned to watch Mrs. DuBois finish chewing Robin out for being such a pitiful rider. *I wonder what she meant by that last comment,* she pondered. *Lord, please keep Sunny and her colt safe. It's funny, I feel almost sorry for Mrs. DuBois.*

They loaded up The Frog and headed for home.

"I am pooped," Jen exclaimed, wiping the sweat beads from her forehead. "I think I'll sleep all the way to Pennsylvania."

Chapter Eleven

"Hey, Jen," Mom called from the living room. "How was the show?"

"It was great," Jen yelled back. She poured herself a tall glass of water and headed toward the direction of Mom's voice.

Mom looked up from her book. "How did Shannon do?"

"She got first place, Mom. I was totally shocked. She was up against ten horses, including one of Mrs. DuBois's students."

Mom's eyes got big. "Shannon beat one of Vanessa DuBois's students?"

Jenny nodded. "It was totally weird, Mom, Mrs. DuBois followed us all the way to Kathy's trailer, screaming at us about how she knew who we where, and how we stole her horse, and then she told me she would make sure I never saw Sunny again. It was creepy. I'm worried about Sunny."

Mom put her book down. "Let's you and I pray right now, Jenny." They held hands and Mom began, "Lord, You can see Sunny and her colt right now. Protect them, Lord, keep them safe. We know that You love these horses too, since You made them. I pray for Jen, that she would have peace and be able to truly enjoy this vacation You have provided for us."

"Amen," agreed Jen.

Mom hugged her. "Why don't you go lie down for a minute. We've got a long trip ahead and you look hot and tired."

"Good idea," Jen said with a yawn. They were still way ahead of schedule. She curled up on her bed, pulling the corner of her comforter over her legs. Her heart beat slowed and her eyelids grew heavy.

She was riding Sunny . . . where? It looked like Sonrise Farm, but there was a house she didn't recognize. And was that a new barn? And Dad? On a horse? It was. He was on a big gray Jenny had never seen before, but it didn't matter. They rode for miles and miles. It was lovely.

They rode back to the barn. Dad helped her with Sunny, and they walked into the house she didn't recognize. It was their house. Mom was there, folding horse blankets.

"Here, Mom, let me help you," she said, reaching out for a blanket.

Jenny woke when her arm moved. She sat there for a moment feeling foolish. She glanced at the clock. Twenty minutes. Strange dream. Perfect nap.

She yawned and stretched. *Let's see, what else do I need to pack?* she asked herself. She stumbled into the living room. She began leafing through the pile of yesterday's mail, hoping to find a current horse magazine to read on the drive. Nothing interesting here, except . . . what is that? It was an official looking letter. It was open.

Jenny sat down on the edge of the old rocking chair.

Dear Mr. and Mrs. Thomas,

I regret to inform you that I have decided to sell my house and property to Fern Castle Development. You will have 90 days from receipt of this letter to vacate the property. You have been excellent renters and I will be glad to furnish you a reference if needed.

Sincerely, Mr. Wellard.

Jen glanced at the date. They got it yesterday! They were going to be homeless!

Mom came in and noticed Jen reading the letter. "Hi sweetie," she said.

"Mom," Jenny whined, holding the letter up accusingly, "I can't believe you didn't tell me about this yesterday!"

"Your Dad didn't even open it until today, Jen. We were *going* to tell you."

"When?"

"In the car, on our trip. We've been expecting this. Mr. Wellard told us when we rented this house a year and a half ago that he was planning to sell. I didn't think you'd be upset."

"Well, I'm just . . . I don't know. I guess I've gotten used to this house, "Jen shrugged. "Where will we go? I don't want to be far from Sonrise Farm."

"The Lord will provide something, Jen." Mom smiled. "In the meantime, it's three whole months away. Let's go to Pennsylvania and have some fun. We could all use a break."

"All right," Jenny agreed. "Let's go."

Mom grabbed her bag and hauled it out the door. Jen pulled her crammed gym bag onto her shoulder. She heaved it into the back of their old station wagon and slammed the door shut. Then she wandered back inside to make one last sweep of her room. *I don't want to forget anything. Lord, help me, have I forgotten anything? Toothbrush, Bible, riding clothes, pj's . . .*

She was headed back through the kitchen, toward the car when the phone rang.

She grabbed it, "Hello, Thomas residence."

Silence . . . static . . .

"Hello," she repeated.

"I need to speak to Jenny," a panicky male voice said.

"Daniel?" she squeaked. "What's wrong? Why are *you* calling me?"

"Aunt Vanessa just came back from a little show," he said breathlessly. "She's ranting and raving about her reputation going down the drain, and how it's all Fire's fault. She got that crooked vet out, they tranquilized the horses and they're taking them. I overheard her; they're driving into the mountains and stopping at a look out point. They're gonna get out of the truck and leave the brake off. The horses will go over the side. Aunt Vanessa will collect the insurance on both of them. She's splitting it with her vet. She's lost it Jen, If you hurry, we can try to stop her. They're just pulling out."

"I'll be there," she promised slamming the phone down. "Lord, help me," she called. "Tell me what to do."

"Dad," she screamed. "Daddy!"

He burst into the room. "What?! Why are you screaming?"

"Dad, Mrs. DuBois was at the show this morning. She recognized me. Daniel just called to tell me that she's planning to kill Sunny and the colt. We need to stop her!"

He didn't question her. "Call, Kathy. I'll call the police on my cell phone."

Her fingers just would not work fast enough. She lost precious moments dialing the wrong number. "Sorry," she apologized to the person on the other end. She dialed again. It rang, and rang, and then Kathy answered.

Kathy gasped loudly at the news. "I'm on my way," she said. "I'll follow her or do whatever I need to do. I have some ideas. Just get out there, Jen!"

Mom prayed out loud as they drove, "Lord Jesus, show us where they are, bring us right to them, Lord."

"Amen," echoed Jen and Dad.

They sped past The DuBois Farm. No sign of her big rig.

"I wonder which way she would go," Dad said out loud.

"Where are the closest mountains?" Jen asked.

"To the west," Dad answered. "Let's turn around."

"What did the police say?" Jen asked.

"They told me to stay in contact, that they were putting three cars on the lookout. It would sure help if we had some idea of their direction. Suddenly Dad turned and glanced at Jen. "I know where they are!"

"Where?"

"There's a place I know where a rig could easily go over. I'll bet that's where they took them. Jen, call Kathy on her cell phone, see where she is."

Jen's fingers trembled as she pressed the little buttons. She got a mechanical voice.

"The customer you are trying to reach is currently unavailable. Please try your call later . . ." She hit the redial button at least ten times. The last time, it rang, then she heard static and snippets of loud voices. "Hello! Kathy, where are you?" Static then silence answered her.

Then the line went dead.

She cradled the phone wishing she could hold on to that momentary sensation of being connected. Their car continued speeding to the west. *Are we going the right way?* she wondered. *What if Dad is wrong? Why haven't we seen them yet?*

Then a thought, and it had to be the Lord, impressed itself in her spinning mind.

I am connected to you and Kathy and Sunny. I am all you need, Jen. Trust Me.

She sat back, allowing the comfort to envelop her. She felt her pounding heart slow to a normal rhythm. *I trust You, Lord,* she said silently—and she did.

As they crested the first mountain, a squad car sped by them, lights and siren blaring. Their old station wagon just couldn't keep up. The road turned to dirt and narrowed. They saw the police car turn off to the right in the distance. Jen just knew it was going where they wanted to be. Her hands hurt from the anticipation. *Is Sunny alive? Is she hurt?*

What about her colt? It was maddening! *If I could just see what's happening!* Jen could feel her heart beginning to pound again.

She closed her eyes, sat back, and began to say over and over, "For I know the plans I have for you, … plans to prosper you and not to harm you ."

Mom chimed in, then Dad, and the Thomas family climbed up the steep mountain road repeating the Lord's promise to Jeremiah together. Jenny felt the truth of the words sink into her soul.

I don't know what we'll find at the top of this road, Lord, but thank You that You already know, and You've got it under control. Please keep Sunny and her colt safe.

An ambulance, heading back down, nearly ran them off the narrow road.

"Oh dear, I wonder who that was," Mom exclaimed, looking back over her shoulder.

They were too late, she just knew it. Jen's eyes filled with tears. There were police cars and rescue equipment everywhere. Yellow warning tape ran clear across the road. She could see the DuBois rig and the two back tires of the stock trailer were hanging precariously over the dropoff. Dad skidded to a halt. "Boy, it's slippery," he said.

Jen flew from the car to see what was happening. Kathy and Daniel sat on the ground near Kathy's truck. "What's going on?" Jen asked breathlessly.

"Oh, Jen, I'm so glad to see you!" Kathy rose and hugged her.

Daniel hopped up. "Hey Jen, we're waiting for a tow truck to drag the truck and stock trailer. If we all stay far away from the trailer the horses are quiet. When we try to get close, they go nuts."

"So what's happening?" Jen asked, wiping away tears of relief. *They haven't gone over . . . yet.*

"Well," Dan started, "I'll tell you the short version. I called you, you called Kathy, Kathy called the police and your vet, Dr. Dave?"

Daniel glanced at Kathy to confirm the name. "Then Kathy drove by and picked me up. We found the rig and were following at a distance. I realized Aunt Vanessa wasn't driving. I ducked down and Kathy passed them to get a look. Aunt V looked like she was sleeping in the front seat. I knew there was no way she'd be asleep right now! We figured Dr. Vaughn was up to something. Fortunately there was enough traffic to let us blend in and follow without him noticing. When he pulled up this road, I knew what he was planning.

"We drove up just as her vet, Dr. Vaughn, was in the process of letting *her* go over the side with the rig. It turns out Aunt Vanessa told him she had put him down as part owner of the colt in exchange for his help in collecting the insurance. He figured he'd get all the money with Aunt V gone."

Jen sat down hard. "Do you mean that you *saved* your Aunt Vanessa?"

"Yup," Daniel answered. "I reached in and set the emergency brake. I had to pull her out. She's on her way to the hospital right now."

"Did she know what was happening?" Jen asked.

"She's sort of awake now. They are taking her in as a

precaution. That vet gave her an injection of horse tranquil-izer."

"And what happens to the horses?"

"We need to get them pulled off that ledge and then, I don't know."

Dr. Dave approached, his face grave. "Jen, the sergeant is of the opinion that these horses need to be euthanized."

"What!"

"That vet, Dr. Vaughn, or whatever his name is, said that they are dangerous to handle, they *do* seem completely trau-matized to me. I can't even get within ten feet of that rig without them almost turning it over. I think putting them to sleep would be kinder than allowing them to fall over the side. Don't you?"

Jen clamped her hand over her mouth, unable to answer such a question.

Daniel stepped forward. "Who actually owns these horses now?" he asked.

One of the police officers overheard the question and walked over. "I'm Officer Gold. I'm new in this state, and each state is different. I can only tell you what I think will happen. The animal warden isn't here yet. I think Mrs. DuBois technically owns them at this time. However, she told us that she never wants to see them again. Dr. Vaughn over there claims he is a partial owner, but even if he is, he has lost custody. He's guilty of attempted murder and ani-mal endangerment. If Dr. Vaughn is an actual part owner or if Mrs. DuBois was involved in the conspiracy, these horses belong to her next of kin."

Daniel shook his head sadly. "She wasn't just *involved,* sir. It was her idea to kill them this way."

"Well, then, I guess we need to find Mrs. DuBois's next of kin. I think they would be the actual owners of these animals. If we can't find the next of kin, the animal warden will have jurisdiction and can award custody to anyone, including himself to give permission to euthanize."

"I'm the next of kin," Dan insisted. "Aunt Vanessa lost her husband years ago and my dad is her only brother."

"Then your dad would be next of kin," the police officer said.

"But he's in California!" Daniel exploded.

"Call him on my cell phone," Kathy said, thrusting the device into his hand.

"I don't want to call him, he hates me," Daniel whispered, pain glistening in his eyes. "He'll probably tell them to kill the horses just to spite me." "Call him," Kathy insisted.

Daniel's shoulders drooped as he punched the numbers. "Hi, Dad?" He walked away from the group, poking his index finger in his ear to hear. He was gone for about fifteen minutes. When he returned his face was glowing. "He is faxing a statement to the police station. It gives *me* custody of the horses. He also said he was so sorry about us. He actually wants me to come home!"

"I'll radio in to the station," Officer Gold said. "As soon as we have your dad's fax, they're yours. I just hope we can get them out of here."

Jenny sidled over to the rig. She saw Sunny's eye peeking out from one of the slats. "Hi, Sunny, remember me?"

The big mare closed her eye slowly.

"You look so tired, sweet girl," Jenny crooned. The horse jerked her lid back up. "It's all right, go to sleep. I'll stay here."

A monstrous diesel tow truck crawled painfully up the steep dirt road. It parked near the police cars. The fire truck stayed on the scene, just in case the rescue went awry. The driver jumped out and began talking to the police. The animal warden pulled up in his green SUV. "What's the story?" he asked.

Officer Gold approached him. The two began conversing with hand gestures. Then the animal warden rummaged about in the back of his truck and emerged with a rifle.

Chapter Twelve

The animal warden marched straight toward the trailer, gun in hand.

"Stop! What are you doing?" Jen almost screamed.

"This is a tranquilizer and these horses are wards of the state. I have jurisdiction over them. This is the only safe way."

"So this is just a dart gun?" Jen started to breathe again. "What about Daniel, doesn't he have custody as next of kin?"

"Not yet, he doesn't. These animals will be impounded then rehabilitated if possible. My guess is that they'll both be put to sleep. They seem extremely dangerous to me."

Dr. Dave ran over. "So, you're going to walk up to two terrified horses and shoot them?"

"Yup, I'll just shoot 'em through the slats."

"What happens when they panic and send the rig over the side, or if they fall near the back of the rig?"

The animal warden scratched his head. "Hmm, didn't think about that. What else can we do? As soon as Lenny starts hooking the tow truck to the rig, they'll flip out. Then we'll lose the tow truck and the rig."

Jen ran to her folks. They were holding hands facing each other, praying. "I'm going to try to get close to the rig, Mom," Jen said, gently touching her mom's arm.

Mom looked startled, "What? I don't think that's a good idea, honey. What happens if it slips over the side?"

"I don't know," Jen admitted, "I just know that nothing else will work. I'm praying that Sunny will recognize and trust me enough to let them hook up the tow truck. I'll stay far away from the back of the rig."

"OK," agreed Dad. "Be very careful."

"Deal!"

An older, white-haired deputy had joined the group of men talking to the animal warden. *He looks familiar,* Jen thought. *Who is that?*

The men walked over to Jenny, intercepting her. The deputy's name badge was visible. *Charlie Smith. He was there the day Sunny . . .*

"Miss Thomas?" inquired the animal warden.

"That's me," Jen said with a nod. "Officer Smith says he knows you and that he's seen you with this horse."

"Yes, sir. He came with Mrs. DuBois to claim Sunny."

"Well, according to him, this horse was fine when she was with you."

Jenny nodded again. "Yes, sir. That is true."

The warden cleared his throat. "Officer Smith has offered to testify in court that the best thing to do for the horses is to release them to your custody. We can sort out the actual ownership details later. Are you willing and able to rehabilitate these horses?"

"Yes, sir!"

"Then I will release them into your custody. If Daniel

turns out to be the rightful owner you will need to give them to him."

"I understand," she nodded. *Nothing matters right now but getting them out of here. At least they won't be put to sleep.*

She approached the stock trailer slowly. She sang Sunny's song, "You are my sunshine, my only sunshine." Sunny moved restlessly causing the trailer to squeak. "Sshhh . . . it's OK, big girl. I'm here."

The mare pricked her ears. Jenny inched a little closer. "You are my sunshine, my only sunshine," she sang quietly. The mare's wild eye softened slightly. Jenny motioned to Lenny to start the hooking up process.

"We're gonna get you out of here," she continued. The colt stamped his feet nervously. The sudden sound made Jenny jump. "Whew," she sighed. "It's nerve- wracking up here."

The tow truck began backing up to the front of Mrs. DuBois's truck. It made a maddening, beep . . . beep . . . beep as it backed. Jenny kept her eyes locked on Sunny's. As long as the mare stayed quiet, the colt did too. Jenny began telling Sunny each step as it happened. She kept her voice low and soft. "Now Lenny is hooking his big truck to your truck. He's going to pull you out of here." Jen glanced toward the front to check on the progress. As soon as she broke eye contact, Sunny began rearing and bucking in place. The colt threw himself against the trailer on the other side. The whole thing began creaking and leaning toward the chasm.

Jenny immediately looked back, "Sunny, Sunny girl. She sang the song as calmly as she could. You are my sunshine, my only sunshine . . ." The horse settled and the trailer grew quiet again.

"OK, I won't look away again, no matter what," she promised the mare. She sang and talked to Sunny from her perch on a stump.

After minutes that seemed like hours, Lenny's strained voice croaked, "We're hooked up. Everybody pray. I'm gonna gun it, so the horses might lose their balance, but it's better than everyone going over the side."

"Lord, keep them safe," Jen begged. She kept her eyes on the mare's eye as she had promised.

Lenny crept quietly into the cab of his truck. He left his door wide open in case he needed to bail out at the last moment. Jen heard the gears grind and complain as he shifted. He revved the motor, then lurched forward. Both horses fell to their knees, then scrambled up.

Lenny did what he'd said. He hauled the rig twenty-five feet before he stopped. He climbed out of his big tow truck shuddering and jerking his shoulders convulsively as he stared at the edge of the steep ravine. "Hate heights, always have, always will. They give me the heebie-jeebies," he growled, rubbing his burly arms as though he'd caught a chill.

Jenny hugged him. "Thank you so much, Mr. Lenny. You saved them."

The animal warden and Charlie Smith walked over to Daniel. Jenny strained to hear the conversation but she stayed next to the trailer as she had promised.

Daniel nodded, then looked around. He saw Jenny and motioned her to him. She shook her head "No" and he jogged over. "The police got the fax from my dad. The horses are now legally mine. What do *you* think we should do with them?"

Jenny thought for a moment. "Daddy, may I use your cell phone?"

He looked surprised for a moment, then handed her the phone.

She ran to the car to grab the directions to Mr. Wright's place. She studied the paper for a moment, then punched the numbers.

"Hello? May I speak to Mr. Wright? OK, could he call me when he gets in? My cell phone number is (703) 555-1234. It's an emergency. Thank you."

She hit the off button and let her arms hang at her side. She felt absolutely spent. Dad walked over and gently took her hand. He pried the phone from her fingers and turned it on. "You want this *on* so he can call you."

She smiled gratefully. "I think we should all go to Mr. Wright's place with the horses. If anyone can help, he can. Let's just start and hope he calls on the way."

"I'll drive Aunt Vanessa's rig," Daniel said. "Jen, do you want to ride with me?"

"Dad, can I?" she begged.

Dad glanced at Mom who nodded slightly. "Are you all packed?"

"Yes, I think I got everything."

"I'm not packed," Daniel said. "And I need to call the farm manager and tell him I won't be there."

"Tell ya' what," Kathy suggested. "Let's go back to Sonrise. I'll get you some of my dad's clothes, Daniel. You can call your aunt's farm manager, we'll grab a snack, make sure the horses have hay and water, and head out."

"Sounds good," Dan agreed.

"We'll follow you," Dad said.

Jen clambered into The DuBois Farm truck, then craned her neck around to peek at Sunny through the slats of the trailer. *She looks all right.* Uncomfortable silence hung like smoke in the cab. Jen stared at her hands, unsure of what to say or think.

"Jen," Daniel started. She looked at him. "I'd like to *give* you Sunny, she's really your horse. I think you should keep her colt too, I'd hate for my aunt to get her hands on him again."

Jenny gasped, shocked. "Daniel, I don't know what to say!"

"Well," he said with a smile, "they're worthless now, on paper anyway. The insurance on them is cancelled and right now they are both fruitcakes. Just between you and me, I'm too afraid of them, and too afraid of what I might do to them. I'd like to go and see Mr. Wright with you. Maybe he can help me become the horse trainer I'd like to be. I'm pretty sure that even Mr. Wright is going to have trouble with these two."

Who cares why he gave them to me. He gave them to me!

"Thank you, Daniel. I will do my best with them." She promised.

As they drove toward Sonrise Farm, Jenny's heart sang. She looked out the back window at the big navy stock trailer with *her* two horses. *Two* horses!

"Dad! Mom! You'll never believe it!" Jenny flung herself into her Dad's strong arms. "Daniel gave me Sunny and the colt! Just like that. He's afraid of his aunt getting them again.

He's going to The DuBois Farm to get the papers. He's going to let the judge sign them over to me! Can you believe it? Sunny and her colt will really be mine!"

"I believe it, Jen," Mom cried joyfully.

The cell phone chirped. It was Mr. Wright. "Hello, Jenny Thomas? I have a message to call you at this number, that it was an emergency. Are you all right?"

"Oh, Mr. Wright, it's incredible. Remember the mare I told you about? Well, the owner *would* like your help." "That's great, Jenny," he replied, clearly puzzled. "Have her call me."

"She did!" Jen crowed.

"I'm sorry, I'm not following you," Mr. Wright said.

"I'm the owner and I called you. We just saved her from . . . it's too long a story. All I want to know is, can we still come tonight and can I bring both of my horses?"

"Absolutely," Mr. Wright answered with a chuckle. "My barn manager just quit. You can help me feed and muck. I'll be expectin' you tonight then. I'll set up a couple mustang pens for your horses."

And they caravaned toward Pennsylvania with Sunny and the colt.

For I know the plans I have for you, . . .plans to prosper you and not to harm you.

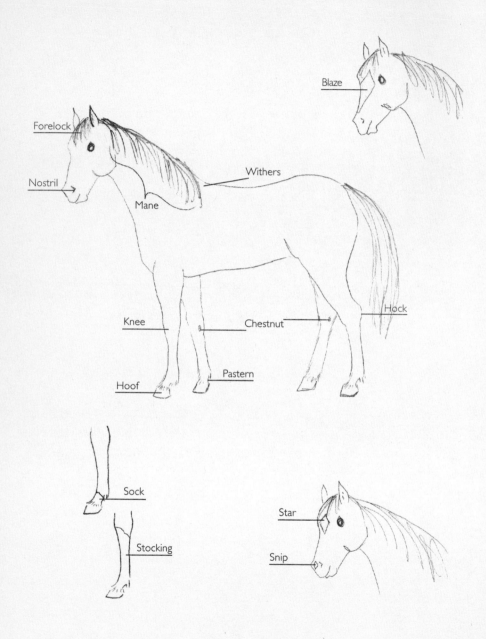

Glossary

A

Arabian—An ancient breed of horse from the deserts of Arabia. Arabians are known for their courage, stamina, and beauty.

B

Bay—A color term for a brown horse whose points (bottom part of legs, mane, and tail) are black. Bays may range from a medium brown to almost black (called a seal bay). A red horse with black points is called a blood bay.

Bridle—The leather straps that fit onto the horse's head to keep the bit in place. The bit is the metal part that goes through the horse's mouth. The reins are the connection to the rider.

Broodmare—A female horse whose job is to have foals (baby horses).

Buckskin—A color term for a light brown horse whose points are black. The color of the body may range from a deep gold to sandy. Buckskins may also have a dorsal stripe (a stripe that runs from wither to tail).

C

Canter—One of the four gaits of a horse. Walk, trot, canter, then gallop. Canter is a three-beat gait, usually smooth and easy to ride.

Chestnut—A color term for a plain red horse.

Clydesdale—One of America's most popular draft (working) horses. Clydesdales are huge, (18 hands or more) powerful work horses used for hauling heavy carts or farm machinery. They are usually bay or black in color, with "feathers" (long hair) covering their hooves.

Colic—A term used to describe stomachache in horses. Colic can be deadly serious or simply a bout of gas that passes on its own.

Colt—A young male horse.

Curry comb—A hard rubber brush used to remove deep or caked-on dirt. It should be used vigorously but carefully, because it is hard. It is not used on the lower part of the legs, nor on the face. Once the dirt has been brought to the surface and loosened, it can be brushed away by the softer bristled body brush.

E

Equine—Scientific name for horses and ponies.

Euthanize—Medical term for destroying an animal. It is usually performed by injecting a deadly substance into the vein. The animal goes to sleep and never wakes. It is painless and fast.

F

Filly—A young female horse.

Foal—A baby horse of either sex.

G

Gelding—A castrated (neutered) male horse. Most male horses in the U.S. are geldings. Only horses intended for breeding are maintained as stallions.

Girth—A leather or fabric belt used to keep the saddle on the horse's back. The girth attaches to both sides of the saddle under the belly of the horse.

Grand Prix—The highest level of competitive show jumping.

Green—An untrained horse.

H

Hands—A measurement term for horses and ponies. Each hand equals four inches. The horse is measured from the ground to the withers (see parts of the horse diagram). A pony who measures ten hands would be forty inches tall at the withers.

Hoofpick—A hand-sized pick used to remove dirt from the inside of a horse's hoof.

Horse—An equine who measures at least 14:2 hands. That is: fourteen hands and two inches. An animal who measures 14:2 would be 58 inches at the withers, or 4 feet, 8 inches. At 17 hands Magnum and Sunny stand 5 feet 8 inches at the withers.

I

Impaction—A serious form of colic where something (food or foreign object) blocks the digestive tract.

Inside and Outside reins—A term used to describe the reins as the horse is moving in a circle. Imagine that you are standing in the center of a ring. There is someone riding clockwise around you. The right side of the horse and rider is visible to you. This is the "inside." The left side of the horse and rider is visible from the fence. This is the "outside." If the horse were to change directions, then the left side would be "inside."

M

Mare—An adult female horse.

Morgan—A small strong American breed of horse descended from Justin Morgan's famous little bay stallion of the late 1700s.

Mucking Out—Cleaning a stall.

Nicker—A low chuckling sound horses make when they see someone or something they love.

P

Paddock—A small enclosure, usually less than an acre in size.

Palomino—A color breed whose coat is the color of a newly minted gold coin. The mane and tail should be platinum.

Platinum—A precious metal that is almost white in color.

Post—The action of rising and sitting in the saddle while your mount is trotting. The reason for posting during the trot is to reduce the jarring that occurs.

R

Ratcatcher—A shirt worn when showing. It has a high collar around the neck and is secured with a bow.

Registered—Each individual breed of horse and pony has a registry, or a list of its members. The registered horses can then trace their ancestry. The Jockey Club of America also requires all racing Thoroughbreds to be tattooed on the inside of the upper lip. This stands as permanent proof of a horse's identity. Sunny, being tattooed, is a registered Thoroughbred. All Jenny needs to do to find Sunny's bloodlines is call the Jockey Club and tell them the number on Sunny's lip. They will be able to look up Sunny's bloodlines.

S

Shy, Spook—The way a horse deals with objects or sounds that frighten him. Shying is ducking sideways suddenly. Spooking is stopping, suddenly, then reacting. It is difficult and unpleasant to ride a spooky horse.

Snaffle—A mild shankless bit that is broken in the middle. The fatter the snaffle, the milder its action.

Stallion—An ungelded (unneutered) adult male horse. Usually difficult to handle.

Stocking—A color term used to describe a leg that is white up to the knee (in front) or the hock (in back). See parts of the horse diagram.

T

Tack—The name given to the collection of stuff that goes on a horse. Saddle, bridle, girth, etc. May also be used as a verb, to mean putting all the stuff onto the horse.

Thoroughbred—A breed of horse known for its long graceful limbs and athletic ability. Thoroughbred horses are used in horse racing.

U

Untack—The act of removing the saddle and bridle from a horse.

W

Weanling—Colts and fillies who are between six and twelve months old. Most horses are removed from their mothers (weaned) at six months. At twelve months of age they are referred to as yearlings.

Welsh Pony—A lovely hardy breed of pony that originated in Wales (a small country next to England).

Whicker—Similar to nicker.

A Sneak Preview
of Book Three in the Sonrise Farm series

Flying High

Jenny slipped from under the thick quilt and pulled on her navy sweats. She padded to the window. The sun was just peeking over the mountaintops; Sunny's pen with its seven-foot fence was barely visible through the trees. Jenny squinted, peering owlishly at first, then smashing her nose against the windowpane. *Where is she?* Leafy branches swayed in the wind hiding a section of the pen. The pen looked empty! *Impossible.*

Jen didn't believe her own eyes. She rushed down the stairs through the back door of the big house. *Now I'm scared,* she realized. The nightmare seemed like nothing. *Sunny is lost in a strange place.*

Dawn was here; the pink light bathed the barn illuminating everything. "Please be there, please be there," she repeated softly, over and over. She tried to keep it at a quick walk but by the time she approached that last corner of the barn, she couldn't stand it. She burst into a full run and flew around the corner.

Empty! The pen was really empty. The gate was closed. *Did she jump? Seven feet?*

The colt startled at Jen's sudden appearance and trotted around his pen, tail high, nostrils flared. *He is breathtaking,* she realized in spite of her panic. "Sorry boy," she whispered. "Did you see where your mama went?"

The colt was indeed staring at something. Jenny followed his gaze and spied Sunny grazing at the edge of the unfenced hay field. Behind Sunny stood thousands of acres of wilderness.

"Sunny," Jen called softly.

The mare popped her head up like a huge frightened deer. Jen could see her ears swiveling around. Sunny looked behind her as though insuring an escape route.

"Oh no sweet girl, you don't want to go there." *Please Lord, don't let her go into the woods.* Jenny looked past the mare at the expanse of property. Mr. Wright had told her last night about the wonderful unspoiled nature of this reserve. The North Mountains and freedom lay behind Sunny. *Will she trust me?*

If you love horses...
Come to Sonrise Farm!

An auction and a jumping competition become the ultimate tests for Jenny's skills, and her faith as well.

Meet Jenny Thomas and her courageous Palomino mare Sunny. Their inspirational adventures are based on true stories, and are sure to inspire horse lovers of all ages. Beautifully written by Katy Pistole, *The Palomino* is the first volume in **The Sonrise Farm series**. *Stolen Gold* is book two and has Sunny in the clutches of an abusive former owner who wants to collect insurance money on the Palomino and her colt. Book three will soon follow. You won't want to miss any of The Sonrise Farm adventures!

Paperback. US$7.99 each.

Ride by and get them at your local Adventist Book Center. Call 1-800-765-6955 or get online and shop our virtual store at www.AdventistBookCenter.com.
- Read a chapter from your favorite book
- Order online
- Sign up for email notices on new products

Prices and availability subject to change.